CLAUDIA,
WHERE
ARE
YOU
?

Hila Colman

CLAUDIA, WHERE ARE YOU ?

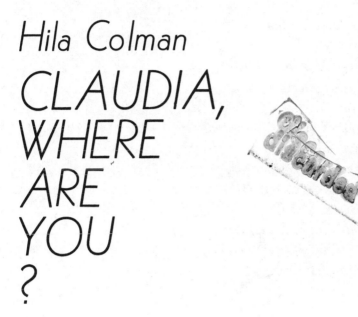

New York   William Morrow and Company

By the Same Author

The Best Wedding Dress
Bride at Eighteen
Car-Crazy Girl
Christmas Cruise
Classmates by Request
A Crown for Gina
The Girl from Puerto Rico
Julie Builds Her Castle
Mixed-Marriage Daughter
Mrs. Darling's Daughter
Phoebe's First Campaign

5   75

FOR BOB AND HIS CLAUDIA

ONE

Of course, there was something wrong with my home life, and with me too no doubt. Girls don't do what I did if everything is groovy and happy in the parents' little nest. What is a happy home and who has one? I suppose that's something for the psychologists to answer, because I'm only a kid and "disturbed" as they say. You know, one of the statistics in the *New York Times* about teen-agers who freak out. But I hadn't planned anything; there was no sinister plot I'd been hiding for months. Anyone could have done it, but I was the one who did. Perhaps that's all there is to it: some people do things and others don't. What I did seems to me very direct and simple with nothing complicated about it.

I have long believed that a lot of things are designed to keep people up tight. That may sound a presumptuous thing to say for someone not yet seventeen, but if you look around the world you'll find that in many places sixteen-year-olds are considered women. Anyway to me Valentine's Day is an event created to make girls nervous. It's almost as bad as Christmas or having your mother make a fuss about a sixteenth birthday. Nothing depresses me more than birthday parties with stupid paper hats, fancy paper napkins, and snappers with dumb messages inside. I mean life can be awful enough without all that phony lovey-dovey stuff in the bargain.

I was thinking about this last February fourteenth when I walked home from school. I just can't believe our town of Stony Point. There's a Main Street, of course, and there are some trees on it, but they don't help. There are also large buckets filled with petunias planted in the spring by the Garden Club ladies, but the effort only makes the shops look more pathetic, like so many forlorn people waiting for a party that never comes off. And, believe me, the valentine decorations, all the hearts and flowers and paper lace and cupids and red bows made the town even worse. Anyone could see that they had come out of moldy boxes for the day and would go back into them again tomorrow. What I mean is, there was nothing gay about the scene.

And I wasn't feeling gay to start with. Not after the conversation I'd had with my mother the night before. My mother is a very nice woman and lots of people like her. The only trouble is she has the wrong kind of daughter. My mother adores sweet-sixteen parties and family Christmases (she gets positively ecstatic if there's snow on the ground and my brother gets home from college by Christmas Eve), and the Valentine's Day dance coming up was another excuse for her to come on strong with her memories. Every year she gives my father hand-painted valentines, which he receives with a large and apologetic grunt, because he usually has forgotten that such a day exists.

So last night she arranged a cozy, fireside-with-hot-cocoa chat with me, her daughter, Claudia. Often these chats revolved around sex, which my mother would be appalled to know is one of her favorite subjects. "Sex," my mother once said to me, "is very beautiful. One day, when you're older, I hope you will know the beauty and joy of making love to a man whom you deeply love and admire. It's nothing to be afraid of."

I didn't answer her at the time, because I was thinking of Roger Ferris. If my mother had ever been kissed by his wet, mushy lips and pulled next to his pimply face, I don't think she would have said that sex is so beautiful. Up to then I had never considered being afraid of sex, but between my mother and Roger Ferris I began to wonder. One of the things I wondered was whether my mother, who always got a funny, nervous expression on her face when she talked about it, wasn't the one who was afraid. Was she trying to convince herself or me that it was supposed to be beautiful? The truth is that I didn't know how I felt about sex, for the very simple reason that all I knew was hearsay, and I had not as yet found anyone whose kisses gave me what my mother called "an inner joy."

On the night before Valentine's Day my mother brought up the subject again, but this time she took a new and different tack. She started off casually asking me if I were going to the dance the next night with Roger Ferris.

"No, I'm not," I told her. We were finishing dinner, and I wanted to get up to my room to play a new record I'd bought.

My mother didn't answer, because she'd gotten pretty smart about not starting those conversations when my father was around. If he heard them at all, and one was never quite sure, he'd be apt to say, "Leave her alone," which, miraculously enough, silenced my mother.

But I could tell by the look on my mother's face that she wasn't finished. Sooner or later she'd come up to my room. The privacy I try to keep in my room is something I'd better explain. Ever since we'd moved (when I was ten) to this ghastly place called Camelot Estates, "a new kind of housing development for discriminating people," I had wanted a lock on my door. You'd think I'd asked to own live snakes, which might not have been such a bad idea, because then my mother would never have come within a mile of my room. But all I'd asked for was a simple, ordinary Yale lock. A terrible commotion ensued. My father said it was a fire hazard and that I could get burned to death if I were locked in my room. My mother said that I would walk off with the key so that our house-keeper Anna could never get in to clean. I told them that I'd climb out the window if there were a fire, and I didn't want anyone in my room to clean it or do anything else. (How gross could they be? The reason I asked for the lock was to keep everyone out.) But I never did get the lock. The only thing that came of the argument was that my mother knocked before she came into my room, which meant nothing because she never waited for me to answer.

Sure enough, that evening there was her little rap-rap, and in she stalked. It is generally agreed that my mother is an attractive woman, that is if you like her silver-manicured nails and her arranged hair, which she has "lightened up occasionally," meaning dyed, of course, a word too honest for her to use. She wears depressingly stylish clothes, and she is the first to tell you that they are months ahead of the fashion. Her excuse for all these "divine" ensembles is the fashion magazine that she works for. "We set the trends," she says with one of her bright little laughs.

"Claudia, dear," she said to me, as I was trying to catch the words on the record, "would you mind turning that music off? I'd like to talk to you."

As always those fatal ominous words caused a hard knot to form in my belly. Claudia, I'd like to talk to you . . . so polite, so modern, so refined. She always spoke according to the articles published in that ladies' magazine of hers, the experts on teen-agers, on infants, on what to do with leftover artichokes, on how to seduce your husband when you're forty, on keeping your skin rosy and your feet adorable, on changing your entire house with a new pillow, on how to guarantee that you'll never get cancer and live happily ever after with a charming daughter, a successful son, and a wonderful husband.

"What's there to talk about?" I turned off the record player and did not push the hair away from my face. If I was sullen looking, it was an automatic reaction beyond control.

My mother gave me one of her winning smiles while she pulled the bedspread over my unmade bed before sitting down on it. "There's always a lot to talk about. Don't you believe that verbal communication raises human beings above the level of animals? The scientists say that dolphins have their own language, which makes them quite as civilized as we are. I believe that if people talked things out the world would be much better off. That's what the U.N. is all about, and if every nation used it we'd have no wars. It seems so obvious to me."

My mother, the world fixer! "If you came up here to have a philosophic discussion with me, I'm not in the mood." Hand-painted Valentines for Kosygin and Mao. . . . I almost giggled at the thought that my mother could be the original flower girl with *Love* written in little hearts across her forehead.

"No, I did not come up here to have a philosophic discussion." She was coming on with the creeping hostility. "I've been worried about you. I know that girls your age want to be left alone, and they do get withdrawn, but there *are* degrees. I . . . the things I want to say are difficult, but I believe in being frank. . . ."

"Go ahead, finish. I'm listening." Surely I could rearrange my records while I listened to her.

"I wish you wouldn't do that while I'm talking. It seems to me that something is worrying you. Believe me, I am not prying. Yet there are areas where I think a mother can be of help. We're running an article in the magazine about . . . well, about what I want to talk about."

"Well, say it. What do you want to talk about?" I let the records sit in a little pile on the floor, not touching them. Her nervousness was tearing me up.

"Actually what I want to talk about is the pill."

I sat frozen.

She went on hurriedly. "I'm not one of those mothers who thinks she should run out and get the pill for her daughter the minute she starts having her period, but I understand you're living in a different age from mine. And I suppose that if a girl is truly in love with a boy, things are different today, and it would be stupid and awful for her to get into trouble. You've seemed so unhappy lately, it occurred to me that perhaps . . . and I wouldn't want you to go to anyone else. After all, that's what mothers are for, to help out. . . . And, well, if you need any medical advice I'd want you to go right over to Dr. Gates, who knows you practically since you were born. I wouldn't have to go with you, if you didn't want me to. But you could talk to him, tell him everything, and I know he'd help you."

I was in a state of shock. "What *are* you talking about?"

"Well, you've been acting so queerly about Roger Ferris. He's an awfully nice boy, and I can see where things you might not have wanted could have happened. Your father and I are not old fuddy-duddies, and we know that things like this have happened since time immemorial. . . ."

"Roger Ferris!" It took me that long to find my voice, and then I shouted out his name. "Roger Ferris!" Suddenly I realized the awful thing she'd been saying to me. "Do you think I went to bed with Roger Ferris?" I wanted to use a dirty, four-letter word, I wanted to be vulgar, to match in some way the low depth of her own mind, but I didn't know how. It was the most repulsive idea I had ever heard in my whole life.

"I don't know that I really seriously thought it, but those things *do* happen. . . ." My mother was stammering, which was not her style.

"I'll tell you one thing," I spoke very distinctly, "if I

ever thought about going to bed with anyone, Roger Ferris would be the very last person in the world I would pick. Now do you mind if I finish playing my record?"

Then my mother got angry. "You have no need to get so excited," she said. "As I said before, I'm not trying to pry into your private life. But, after all, you're only sixteen and there are some things that a mother must know. Some things are important, Claudia, even if you and your generation don't think they are. By the way, did you call Mrs. Matthews?" It was typical of her to switch the conversation suddenly when it got sticky for her, and when she did to pick the most unpleasant subject possible.

"No I did not call Mrs. Matthews. And you may as well know now, I never will."

My mother stared at me speechless, but what she was thinking showed in her eyes. "Ungrateful, after all I've done for you, I'm working so hard to give you and your brother every advantage, you're making a fool of me, the least you can do is pick up the telephone, Mrs. Matthews is a very important person on our magazine and a close personal friend, you'd think I'd suggested something awful, taking a summer job in our college and career department, why girls from all over the country would give their right arm to be considered. . . ." Every word, every phrase had been said to me in the past few weeks. Spoken, hurled, thrust, cajoled, threatened, entreated. . . .

"You do not seem to understand that I do not wish to work for *Woman Beautiful* this summer or any other time. That's that." We continued to stare at each other like two enemies across the firing line. A shot either way would have been a relief.

"I'll tell you one thing. You're not going to sit around here and mope all summer. I've had enough of that this winter." My mother was assembling her artillery.

"You're not here to watch me anyway, so what do you care?" My thrust was clean and neat. "Don't blow your cool," I added with a final burst of fire. "I'll be someplace else, so you won't have to worry."

"And where will you be? If you think we're going to send you off to Europe, you're very much mistaken. Your father and I think you should work this summer and earn some money toward your college education. That is, if you get into any college next fall," she added haughtily.

I smiled. The whole argument was so ridiculous. We were two people discussing trivia when one of us was going to throttle the other. And damn it, I wasn't going to be done in. I wasn't a piece of sweet butter that she was going to pat into one of her fancy molds and serve up with a gleam in her eye for her friends to admire.

"If you want me to go to college, you'd better let me do my homework," I said calmly. What else could she do, but walk out of the room?

When I closed the door behind her (typically she had left it wide open), I turned on the record player and lay down on my bed. I was utterly exhausted and felt that if only I could sleep for a million hours maybe I'd have the strength to think. I didn't have any homework, and if I had I wouldn't have done it. I just lay there immobilized, trying to grab hold of something real out of the amorphous but enormously heavy layers of fog I was immersed in.

Nothing was what it seemed to be. Money, for instance. In our family there was money for everything and money for nothing. My mother and father talked about money a great deal. Could they afford this or that? Something was expensive or something was a bargain. But nothing they said made any sense to me. A hundred-dollar Lowestoft dish that my mother never used was a bargain, but if I had some girls over for supper, shell steak was too expensive, so we had to have hamburgers. Two or three pounds of steak would have cost less than five dollars. They had money for a gardener, but I got nagged about weeding, and more often than not when I wanted something it was "too expensive." I mean what's the sense in having money if everyone in the family can't enjoy it?

Of course, they had plenty of money for my college. I didn't mind getting a job if it was something I wanted to do, but to say that I needed the money for college was so much garbage. Besides lying to me they lied to each other about money. I knew that my mother never told my father the truth about what she paid for her clothes, and he was just as bad when he bought a new set of golf clubs.

My brother Edward didn't feel about money the way I did. He took all he could get and constantly asked for more. I thought it was pretty disgusting, since he didn't think any more of my parents than I did, and wasn't any closer to them either. He was just out for himself. Security for him was a wallet stuffed with crisp ten-dollar bills, although he was always broke, and not what I would call happy.

I hated the games my parents played, and I didn't want any part of their money or their college or even their shell steaks, which I didn't get when I wanted them anyway. Most of the things around me were phony; nothing was what it seemed to be. Our house was made of something that was supposed to look like fieldstone, but wasn't; our television set looked like an old Spanish treasure chest;

my mother had an assortment of wigs for *apres* swimming; my father wore turtleneck shirts to hide the wrinkles on his neck; our sunroom was filled with terribly expensive fake tropical trees.

I was thinking about all this when I walked home from school on Valentine's Day, and all those flowery decorations struck me as being more of the same. As far as I knew Valentine's Day, after all these years, had never made anyone more loving. Mrs. Kelly, who owned the beauty parlor, had a scowl on her face, because her husband was in the bar a few blocks down getting drunk. Mr. Greenbaum, in the shoe store, looked miserable because his daughter had run off to marry a *goy*. The Esposito sisters, in the Gourmet shop, were pretending to look pleasant, but the minute the customers left they'd be fighting again. So what was the good of all those banners of love?

When I got home Cynthia called me. She asked me if I was going to the dance that night.

"No," I told her, "I'm not."

"But I thought Roger asked you."

"He did, but I'm not going."

"Oh, Claudia, I wish you would. It'll probably be boring, but there's nothing else to do around here, and at least if you come the four of us can have some fun. Please."

"I'm sorry, but I can't. I don't feel like it. You'll have a good time with Fred."

"What's the matter? Are you all right? You sound depressed."

"No more than usual. You can tell me all about the dance tomorrow."

Roger Ferris! Cynthia had to remind me! My mother's gross insinuation the night before gave me goose pimples. How could she have been living in the same house with me all those years and even think that I would do such a thing—and with Roger Ferris! The fantastic fact that she knew me so little was even worse than the things she had said. It was as if suddenly all the fake trimmings of our family life had been torn down, and I was facing a moment of truth. I was a stranger in my own home.

Sitting in my room, I could imagine my mother calling out in her usual way when she came home, "Claudia, where are you?" As if knowing whether I was at my desk or in the bathroom made any difference, when the naked truth was she never knew where the inside me, my thoughts, the important Claudia, not just my body, ever was. I guess I made up my mind then that I couldn't bear it any longer, that I wouldn't be there when she came home, or tomorrow either.

For some reason, perhaps to be nice, I straightened up my room and waited until I heard Anna go upstairs for her afternoon nap. Then I went downstairs and quietly walked out of the house.

TWO

The 5:22 out of Grand Central Station was already crowded when Jean Nichols walked into the club car, a pale pink knit (Pauline Trigère) under her furs and a trail of expensive fragrance floating behind her. A smile lightened her pretty and expertly made-up face when her eyes found her husband and saw that he was saving a seat for her. She placed the oblong box she was carrying on the floor, close to her knees, and gratefully sank down beside him.

"I thought I'd never make it. Why do crises always happen at five o'clock? This time it was those pictures we spent all yesterday taking. They're no good. We have to do the whole job over again. I don't know why they couldn't have waited until tomorrow morning to show them to me." She opened up her mink coat and settled herself comfortably in her seat. "How was your day, dear?"

David Nichols looked up from his newspaper. "Nothing much. I had to spend the morning in court. Lloyd was sick."

"That's a pity. I know how you hate going to court. It never ceases to amaze me. I should think that would be the most exciting part about being a lawyer. It's so dramatic. But then I'm an extrovert and you're an introvert." She changed the subject then. "I'm bringing home a really lovely dress for Claudia to wear to the dance tonight."

"Is she going to a dance?"

"Yes, of course. It's Valentine's Day. Didn't you. . . ."

David Nichols turned around so that he could pat his wife's arm. "Yes, of course, Mrs. Jacobs put your lovely valentine right next to some flowers on my desk. Did you send the flowers too?" He had a quizzical smile on his face.

Mrs. Nichols shook her head. "No, she must have bought them. How sweet of her."

"I'm sorry, dear. You know I always forget these things. You deserve to be married to a man who remembers valentines and anniversaries. . . ."

"I'm not complaining," Mrs. Nichols said, but there was a wistful expression on her face as she looked out the window. She shook the sleeve of her coat where she had been leaning on it. "How can I complain when I look out at that?" she added, watching the dark, shoddy, dismal tenements of Harlem go by. "I wish Claudia would feel the same way. She has so much, and she seems so unhappy. . . ."

"What happened last night?" Mr. Nichols was turning to a back page of the paper as he asked the question. "She looked as if she'd been crying. What did you and she talk about upstairs?"

Mrs. Nichols flushed, but her husband didn't notice. "Oh, nothing. Just girl talk. Although that's hard to come by with Claudia. She's so close-mouthed. I wish she opened up more."

"You worry about her too much. Girls her age aren't supposed to confide in their mothers, are they?"

"But I'm not an ordinary mother," Mrs. Nichols said indignantly. "At least, I try not to be. I know what's going on, and I think I know girls and women. That's my business after all. I'm no prim Victorian. If Claudia would only talk to me, I'm sure I could help her."

"Maybe, maybe not." Mr. Nichols went on reading his paper.

Mrs. Nichols thought about the dress she was bringing home for her daughter. Getting it had been no easy feat, for it had involved a tedious trip crosstown from her Madison Avenue office through a lot of traffic to Seventh Avenue. Then she had to cajole the wholesaler into letting her walk off with his sample model in exchange for the promise of pictures of her daughter wearing it. Her next problem would be to get Claudia to agree to the pictures, which, knowing Claudia as she did, would present another hurdle. But the dress was perfect, a wild print that Claudia would look marvelous in, and if she read it as a peace offering after last night. . . . Well, what was the harm in that?

"Do you want a drink?" Mr. Nichols asked.

"Yes, I'd love one."

Sipping her vodka martini, Mrs. Nichols set herself to relaxing while the train carried her home. She was quite proud that she had taught herself to make use of whatever scarce free moments she was able to snatch in her complicated and harried life. At least once a day, she closed her door and stretched out on the chaise longue in her office, leaving instructions with her secretary not to be disturbed. During these sessions Mrs. Nichols had formed the habit of reviewing whatever positive accomplishments she had achieved earlier. Jean Nichols was a firm believer in positive thinking. Obstinately she ignored those things that were distasteful and comforted herself with those that were pleasant.

Her method had proved successful. In her early years she had learned to look beyond the squalor and poverty of the depression in which she had grown up and to equip herself for a finer existence. As a child she used to lie in her sunless, bare room, close her eyes, and imagine herself another Cinderella. And she made her dream work. Fresh out of high school, she started off as a young copywriter on an insignificant trade magazine. Little by little she worked herself up to what she was today, the executive editor of an important national magazine for "younger women." Along the way she also had found David, a highly eligible young lawyer, and in hard-won, but confident steps she had moved herself from the New

York tenement where she was born to the spacious ten-room house in Stony Point, Connecticut. Whatever was missing in her life, she continued to ignore.

She liked to talk, but David didn't. As a result, she had learned to rely on her own thoughts and fantasies much of the time they were together. Now she was going over the day's scoreboard. In spite of the last-minute crisis, it had not been a bad one.

The staff meeting for the August issue, which was to be built around the theme of getting the children back to school, and facing the joys of a house alone once again, had gone well. Jean Nichols's philosophy of looking on the bright side overflowed onto the pages of her magazine, for she believed that in exchange for their money her readers deserved to be cheered up.

"We'll be alone next September, won't we?" she said suddenly to her husband.

"What do you mean?"

"Both Claudia and Edward will be away at college. There'll be just the two of us."

"What made you think of that?"

"We're running our August issue around that theme. An empty nest and how to fill it."

"That's one thing you don't have to worry about," her husband told her.

"No, I guess not," Mrs. Nichols said, but she was quite unprepared for the sharp, forlorn feeling she had at the thought of a house without either of her children in it. Loneliness was a subject she shied away from. A woman with a job, a husband, and a family had no right to be lonely, and she never admitted that she sometimes felt a desperate yearning for a close companion, someone she could really talk to. All during the staff meeting she had presented many good reasons why a woman would enjoy having her house to herself. But now the thought that she was also talking about her own home was disturbing. Although she realized that her relationship with her daughter had been far from close for some time, the fact that Claudia was home permitted Mrs. Nichols to indulge in some wishful, gay dreams. Perhaps Claudia would give a party or invite a young man to dinner. . . .

Bleak thoughts were not constructive. Mrs. Nichols searched her mind for a happier prospect than an empty house and hit upon the appealing idea that a daughter in college could bring its own pleasures. Pleasures she had never known but had longed for. There would be the fun of getting together a marvelous wardrobe for Claudia, driving up to some charming New England campus, giving parties at home for Claudia's new friends, enjoying the vicarious excitement of the football games and proms and winter carnivals Claudia would be going to. Perhaps Claudia would join a sorority. . . .

By the time they reached Stony Point Mrs. Nichols had many additional ideas for the magazine and had happily decided that if Claudia and she didn't see each other daily their relationship might improve. They might even achieve the healthy, intimate friendship that the magazine espoused. Perhaps she would write an editorial about it . . . when your daughter leaves home may be the time you get to know each other best . . . enjoy your children when they are away at school. . . . The idea was a good one and thinking about it was comforting.

"Come on, dear. Let's walk to the back of the car. Don't forget your package." Mr. Nichols hustled his wife out of the train.

"What's on for tonight?" he asked, as he started up the Mercedes. "I'm sure you told me, but you know I forget these things."

"That young couple I told you about, the McRoberts, are coming to dinner. But I made it late," she added hastily, "so you'll have time for a nap. Nancy is the new girl in our career department. Terribly attractive and bright. I thought it would be good for Claudia to meet her. I think her husband is some kind of an expert with a computer or something. They have a house not too far from here."

"Doesn't sound like Claudia's dish. Thought you said she was going to a dance."

"Yes, but that's not until later. She won't be going until after dinner, around ten or so I imagine. I think it's important for Claudia to know that not all young people are alienated. Nancy has a purpose in life. And she adores her mother. Speaks about her all the time." Mrs. Nichols took out a mirror from her alligator handbag and smoothed down her hair.

"How old is this Nancy?"

"About twenty-four I guess."

"That's a little different from sixteen. Does her mother live with her?" Mr. Nichols pulled the car into the graveled driveway.

"Oh no. Her mother's back home in Iowa or some such place."

"She can afford to adore her then," Mr. Nichols commented.

Mrs. Nichols got out of the car without answering. Her husband's implication that all daughters had to rebel against their mothers was upsetting; she knew more about that subject than he did, and besides she envisioned herself as no ordinary mother. Young women and young girls wrote to her from every part of the country asking for advice: surely her own daughter could take advantage of her knowledge and experience. She only wanted a full and happy life for Claudia, the wonderful, young-girl things she never had known.

"Claudia, where are you?" Mrs. Nichols called into the empty hallway. Hearing no answer, she went on into the kitchen to ask Anna where Claudia was.

"I think I heard her go out a while ago after she came home from school."

"Did she say when she'd be home?"

"No, I didn't see her. I was up in my room."

"Did the flowers come?"

"Yes, ma'am. They're here."

"Good. I'll be down in a few minutes to arrange them. Bring in the big bowls from the living room, please." She followed her husband upstairs. "Are you going to lie down?"

"I may as well. Wake me up in time before your guests arrive."

"You mean *our* guests," his wife corrected him.

In a few minutes Mrs. Nichols had changed out of her city clothes and into a long, silk kaftan that she wore at home. Down in the large, pine-paneled kitchen she chatted with Anna and arranged her flowers.

Her eyes kept going to the clock. "I wonder where Claudia is. She should be home having a rest before going to the dance tonight. I brought a marvelous new dress home for her, and I'm dying to see how she looks in it."

"She's a lucky girl the way you buy things for her," Anna said.

"I enjoy doing it. And why not? She's the only daughter I have. I wish she liked clothes more, though. She never wears that cashmere sweater I gave her for Christmas." Mrs. Nichols had a frown between her eyes, but her voice was wistful.

"The kids today have too much. They don't appreciate anything anymore." Anna firmly put the finishing touches on a pie.

"Some kids have too much, and some don't have enough. That's the trouble." Mrs. Nichols stood back to admire her flowers. "There, I think they look all right. Anna, put the low bowl on the dining-room table, and the others back in the living room, please."

"I wonder where Claudia can be," Mrs. Nichols said a little later to her husband, just a few minutes before their guests were due. "That girl has no sense of time. I told her this morning that the McRoberts were coming. You'd think she could get home on time. I don't want to keep dinner waiting. It's not fair to Anna."

"Call up Cynthia. Maybe she's over there," Mr. Nichols suggested.

"I'm not going to call up after her. She's a big enough girl to know when to come home. This kind of irresponsibility really gets me angry. The least she could do would be to telephone and say she was going to be late."

"You're right," Mr. Nichols agreed. "If she comes in too late, I think you ought to keep her home from the dance tonight."

Mrs. Nichols was shocked. "Oh, I couldn't do that." And then she laughed. "I'd be depriving myself as much as Claudia. I love to see her go out and have a good time. No, I'll just talk to her. She's too old for that kind of punishment anyway."

"Suit yourself."

Mrs. Nichols sighed. Long ago her husband had acknowledged that the bringing up of their two children was her department. When they were young, she had welcomed the free hand, because he and she had not always agreed, and Mrs. Nichols thought the children should not be subjected to differing points of view. But as

Claudia and Edward grew older she often longed for a full-dress discussion with her husband on the children's problems; Mr. Nichols, however, continued to avoid it, saying she was the expert. That both parents should be involved in raising their children was a favorite theme of the magazine, and she was sensitive about the fact that she had never achieved this relationship in her own home.

"I hope she doesn't come home in one of her awful, teen-age moods." Mrs. Nichols took the new dress out of its box, put it on a hanger, and admired it. "It's so pretty! I'll put it in Claudia's room as a surprise." She was trying very hard to keep her cool, as Claudia would put it, because she didn't want to spoil the evening for Claudia by having an argument before the dance.

Claudia's room looked strange. And then Mrs. Nichols noticed that the bed was made and the desk neat. Even the top of the bureau was tidied up. "Well, this is a switch," Mrs. Nichols said to herself. She hung the dress on the outside of the closet, so that Claudia would see it first when she came into the room. Taking a piece of paper from Claudia's desk, she made a big heart on it with a red pencil, wrote across it, *Happy Saint Valentine's Day*, and pinned the note to the dress. The dress looked stunning, and she was torn between a flow of warm emotion for the girl who had cleaned up her room so nicely, the pretty girl who would be going to a dance in a pretty dress that night, and a rising anger against the girl who had not come home to throw her arms around her mother and to love the dress.

Just as Mrs. Nichols was about to leave the room, a white envelope on Claudia's bureau caught her eye. It had no stamp on it, and she stopped to take a look. The second she saw the words *Mom and Dad* penciled across it in Claudia's handwriting her heart skipped a beat. She stared at the square envelope unable to open it, filled with a terrible premonition of disaster. She leaned against the bureau to steady herself, her eyes searching the room quickly for some reassurance before she opened this thing that seemed to be burning her hand. The neatness of the room now was frightening. The extravagant red and orange Italian bedspread, which Claudia had disdained to use, complaining it was too heavy to move, was carefully smoothed into place. The blue blotter on her desk was cleared of its usual messy pile of papers and books. The unopened bottles and jars of cosmetics that Mrs. Nichols continually brought home from the office were in two neat rows on the dressing table. There were no clothes on the floor or draped over the two chairs. It was a room empty of its occupant. Nobody lived in it.

"David! David, come here!" Mrs. Nichols's voice was shrill.

"What's the matter?" Mr. Nichols came into the room putting on his blue blazer.

"Here, open this." She handed him the envelope.

Barely glancing at the outside, Mr. Nichols ripped open the letter. He read it to himself quickly and handed it to her silently.

Mrs. Nichols read Claudia's note:

Dear Mom and Dad,

I have left home. I need to get away. Please do not worry about me. I will be all right. And *please* do not try to find me. I need to be alone for a while. Later I'll get in touch with you.

Claudia

Mrs. Nichols read the note twice before she lifted her face and looked into her husband's eyes. "David, what should we do?" Her face was pale and stricken, her voice filled with emotion.

"I don't know. I just don't know." He sounded helpless and stunned.

"Oh, David. . . ." Mrs. Nichols turned to her husband, sobbing. "What has happened? I don't understand it, I just don't understand it."

"I'm afraid that's it," he said gently. "We don't understand it. We don't understand Claudia. We don't understand the whole generation."

Mrs. Nichols shook her head impatiently. "I hate these generalities. They don't apply to us. Claudia doesn't come from a broken home. We're one of the few couples we know who've only been married to each other. We don't fight, we're not drunks, we've done everything we could. Maybe she doesn't understand us," she added almost angrily. "What should we do, David?" she asked, her voice breaking again.

"I don't know. I guess nothing right now." He picked up the note and read it again. "Maybe she's just gone off to be with one of her friends for a few days. I think we have to sit tight and hope we'll hear from her in a couple of days."

"But she's so young, only sixteen. Anything can happen to her." Mrs. Nichols was crying again.

"She's a pretty sensible girl. I don't think she'd do anything. . . ." His choked voice belied his attempt to remain calm.

"I'm going to call Edward. Maybe he knows where she

is." Mrs. Nichols felt some relief that she had thought of something to do right away. She dialed the phone in Claudia's room, but there was no answer in Edward's off-campus apartment near his university.

At that moment the bell rang. "Oh, dear God, it must be the McRoberts! I forgot about them." Mrs. Nichols looked at herself in Claudia's mirror, smoothed down her hair, and put some of the powder on Claudia's dressing table on her face. "Let's not talk about this tonight, please. We'll just say that Claudia's out. All right?" She had to struggle to keep herself from breaking down again.

"If that's what you want, of course."

She shrugged her shoulders in a helpless gesture. "What else can we do? If it really is nothing and will blow over in a couple of days, I'd rather people didn't know about it. I feel so terrible . . . my own daughter. . . . I only hope I can stay calm."

THREE

I could see the lights in the school as I walked down the hill from my house. My friends (Do I have any real friends?) were putting up their paper decorations, making jokes, giggling, pretending to have fun, when all the time they knew, as well as I, that the dance was going to be a dud. The only fun would be afterward. When the dance was over, or while it was going on, couples would be making out in someone's car. Some of the girls went the limit, even, I think, my friend Ellen. My mother adores Ellen. She thinks she is so charming and poised and refined.

She should know some of the things about Ellen that I do. Of course, Ellen never told me everything, I don't think anyone ever does, but I'd watched her in action plenty of times, opening her blouse practically down to her waist, tightening her jeans so she couldn't breathe, disappearing for hours at a party. The boys she disappeared with were not the kind who sat and talked about life; they were out for one thing, and I'm sure charming Ellen gave it to them.

But I wasn't thinking about Ellen that night. My mind was on myself. It was a hideously cold night. I had my overnight bag with me, and it wasn't easy to keep walking down the hill to the station with the wind whipping through my old Loden coat, and nothing between me and it but my thin tights and a short skirt. To suit the mood I was in, I had put on old clothes, and I was kind of sorry I had left my new, warm, fake-fur coat at home. Although I guess under no conditions would I have taken it. It was one of the things my mother had brought home for me from the magazine or from some great friend of hers on Seventh Avenue. To me, it looked like Miss Junior Miss from Best and Company. I guess I have a thing about clothes. I hate spending money, any real money that is, on them. It seems such a waste on me, as if it would make any difference what I wore.

Any slight thought I might have had about turning back and going home certainly got lost when I went past Dorothy Blake's house. Actually I didn't go by it, but quickly darted around the corner and went the long way around. Her house was lit up like a Christmas tree, and I remembered that she was giving a dinner party before the dance. And who should be parking his car in the driveway but pimply faced Roger Ferris.

Believe me I didn't give a damn about Roger Ferris, and I didn't care who he saw, because he's the original creep. But the truth was that not even he had asked me to the dance. Not even Roger Ferris had invited me.

When I first started dating Roger, Cynthia and my mother kept telling me how attractive he was, but I knew better. No one attractive was dating me because I was a mess. My mother could tell me ten million times that I was pretty, but I knew she was lying. I could see it in her eyes and by the way she constantly made casual little suggestions and dropped her *Woman Beautiful* hints on how to make myself more attractive. The way she raved about the girls in her office and how stunning they were

—sometimes I actually felt sorry for her, because she had an ugly daughter. I am tall and skinny, and in damp weather my hair curls up instead of lying flat and straight. I'm not pretty and pert like Ellen or dark, moody, and romantic like Cynthia. My face is so ordinary. I have two blue eyes, a nose and a mouth—my eyelashes are pretty good; they're dark and kind of long—but my mouth is too big and my eyes too wide apart, and my nose a little crooked. My figure barely fills out my bra while Ellen wears a B cup already. I hate the way I look, and I don't know how to put on an act. I mean Roger Ferris knew right away that I didn't like his kissing me, although Cynthia said I would get used to it, and I was a fool not to pretend that I was having a glorious time.

But when Roger came up close to me and I could feel and smell him breathing on my face, and he made all those funny noises as if he were running for a train, and he tried to open my mouth with his tongue, I couldn't think of anything except pushing him away. I did try to let him alone a few times, but it was no use. I'm simply no actress, and if that's what you have to do to get invited out, I'm a flop and that's all there is to it. I'd rather stay home, except that there my mother was nagging me all the time to do this or that, to change my hair or put on lipstick, so that I'd be popular. All she had to do was to look at me and know why I wasn't, that nothing in the world except a new face and figure would do any good.

So when I saw Roger Ferris going into Dorothy's house I felt really swamped by my depression. I knew then that I didn't belong anywhere in Stony Point and that I had to get out before I took an overdose of sleeping pills the way Julie Hammond did her senior year at college. Believe me I had thought of it, but I guess I was curious about what was going to happen to me if I lived.

So I kept on walking to the station. I was worried that some of the kids would see me and ask me where I was going, but I had a story that I was going to New York to see my grandmother ready for them. It's a pretty long walk from our house to the station, and it was getting dark already, the way it does in February around five thirty, and the wind was awful, but the darkness was a relief because I felt less conspicuous in it. I ducked around the back streets, because I didn't want to go down Main Street, past the shops, and run into people who knew me. Then, as I got near the station, I saw Mrs. Caldwell drive up and park her car and I knew right away that she was going down to New York on the same train that I was. She's a friend of my mother's, so of course I didn't want to run into her.

At that point I got panicky. I don't know what I thought she would have done to stop me, but all dressed up in her fur coat and huge fur hat, she seemed like some mammoth creature who would bear down and swallow me up. Maybe my reaction was a symbolic kind of thing, because Mrs. Caldwell represented everything that I loathed about Stony Point and my own home. Frantically I made a dash for the back end of the station, flew into the ladies' room, and locked the door.

I don't know who uses the john at the station. I'd never been in it before, and I don't know anyone who ever has, and I soon discovered why. It was small, dark, smelly, and dirty. It was horrible in there, and I was worried about getting out in time to buy a ticket and still avoiding Mrs. Caldwell. I tried peering out the filthy small window, but I couldn't see anything except the lights of cars going by. Thank goodness I had my watch, so I stood there, staring at my watch, counting the minutes until the train was due.

At last I took a chance and opened the door a tiny bit. There were a few people in the station, but I didn't see Mrs. Caldwell, so I came out. Luck was with me, because she must have gone outside to walk down the platform to the front end of the train where most people like to ride so they'll be nearer the exit when they get out at Grand

Central. I bought my one-way ticket quickly (the station man gave me a funny look when I said I didn't want a round trip) and went outside to the back end of the station. Finally I heard the whistle of the train as it came around the bend and heaved a big sigh of relief.

When the train pulled out of the station, and I was on it, I began to get terribly excited. The car was almost empty, and I had a seat to myself by the window. There's one little place past Mr. Green's warehouse where you can see the school from the train, and I blew it a kiss good-bye. Good-bye and good riddance, I thought to myself. Good-bye to Stony Point, good-bye to everything. I wasn't scared anymore. I felt marvelous. I was on my way. Oh, beautiful!

On the ride down I wondered why I hadn't left before. It seemed the obvious thing to do. If you hate being in a place—get up and walk out. I didn't think of myself as a runaway, like so many kids, because I wasn't going away for kicks. I had a purpose. And I did have a sort of plan. There was this girl, Myrna Lowe, who had graduated two years ahead of me. She had an apartment down in the Village and was working in New York. We had never been terribly good friends, but I'd seen her a few times when she'd come home for holidays or weekends, and she always said why didn't I come down to New York and stay over with her. We weren't intimate, but we liked each other. She hated Stony Point as much as I did, and the minute she graduated from high school she left home. I think she went to art school for a while, but she had a job now, and being nineteen she was very much on her own. I figured I'd call her as soon as I got to New York. I had about fifty dollars with me, money left over from Christmas, so if I could stay at Myrna's for a while, I thought I'd have enough until I figured things out and looked over the scene.

On the way down we passed a train going up north, and I realized my parents were probably on it. The train was crowded, and I knew they'd be in the club car having a drink, as they always did, not knowing there was a surprise waiting for them at home. All I felt was a great relief that I wasn't going to have to sit through a dinner with that girl from the office my mother had told me about, another one of her glamour girls, who was gorgeous and bright and would be putting on all evening, asking me stupid questions about school and what I wanted to do. I knew I would detest her. I can't stand the women from my mother's office. They try to draw me out because they think they've found a real teen-age contact for the phony stuff they put in their magazine.

When I got to Grand Central, I stopped to buy a bar of

chocolate—I was starving by then—and went to the ladies' room. By this time I really had to use it, and then I called Myrna's number. I let the phone ring and ring, but there wasn't any answer. Maybe she wasn't home from work yet I thought, so I walked around the station for a while, and then came back to the phone in the ladies' room again. But still there wasn't any answer. I sat down and waited. I guess I dialed that number a dozen times, forcing myself to wait five minutes in between, but Myrna wasn't home.

I couldn't stand that station any longer, so still carrying that overnight bag of mine I went outside. It was just as cold in New York as it had been in Stony Point, and if anything the wind was worse. I walked down 42nd Street, and went past a movie, some monstrous nudie. There was a big line outside, and besides it cost two and a half dollars, which I wouldn't spend for something good, so I didn't try to go inside. Every few minutes I went into a phone booth to call Myrna and to get out of the wind, but still there was no answer. I didn't know what to do, so I went back to the station.

This time several nuns were in the ladies' room, and the way they were sitting there—so placidly with their scrubbed, serene faces, as if nothing in the world was worth getting bothered about—gave me an odd kind of comfort. I felt that if I sat down near them, nothing could happen to me, although I was beginning to feel kind of frantic and frightened. When they got up to leave I left too, and sick of dialing Myrna's number I decided to take the subway down to where she lived on MacDougal Street.

I got out of the subway at Astor Place and walked west and then across Washington Square Park to Mac-Dougal Street. The last time I'd seen the park had been in September, when it was still warm and the place was filled with kids, some playing guitars and singing. But there was hardly anyone in it now, except some couples walking their dogs. Everything seemed sad. I sat down on a bench for a few minutes—I was so tired—and wondered if I'd die of the cold if I had to sit there all night. Maybe a cop would pick me up. I pulled my coat close around me, listening to the city, looking up at the bare trees, and suddenly it was very quiet. I thought about a quiet little place in the forest I used to go to when I was a kid at camp.

I didn't like camp. I hated athletics. I couldn't do anything well, even throw a ball, and I hated having to sleep in a room with a bunch of other kids. So I used to sneak out to this little place in the woods, where there was a big rock in a tiny clearing. Through the trees I could see a tiny patch of the blue lake. My counselor used to get furious with me for disappearing and accused me of all kinds of disgusting things, things I didn't even understand at the time, but all I did was to sit there and have a lovely time making up stories about a fairy queen giving me three wishes, and I kept changing what those wishes would be. While I was in the clearing I felt a sadness as if I were the only person left in the whole world and all the animals in the forest were counting on me to stay alive and save them.

I felt that same sadness then, sitting alone in Washington Square Park. There was something extraordinary and special about being alone, but the responsibility of my aloneness was awful; if something happened to me I felt I would be betraying a lot of other people. None of it made any sense, and I didn't try to understand it, but the feeling was very strong.

I looked up at the lights in the apartments around the square, and I wondered if there were any kids in those buildings having a good time. Then I thought of the valentine dance and of Roger Ferris, and I decided that probably no one ever had a good time. Except maybe if a girl were with someone terrific. . . . Would I ever find the person to be close to? Was there any boy alive who could understand and know everything without my needing to tell him?

MacDougal Street that night wasn't lively and noisy, the way I remembered it, just a few kids in doorways and on the street, shivering from the cold. I walked past Myrna's house a few times before I could find the number, and I buzzed and buzzed her bell, but all I could hear was the forlorn ringing of a bell in an empty apartment.

I was cold and tired and scared. In the back of my mind was the thought that as a last resort I could call up my grandmother, but then I'd be right where I was before and didn't want to be. I walked back along Mac-Dougal Street and went into a coffee shop. It was warm in there and a few hippie kids were sitting at a table, but watching them laughing and talking with each other I felt lonelier than ever. I wouldn't even fit in with them. Myrna had told me that finding a place to sleep in a crash pad was easy, but that was mostly in the East Village, and besides I simply didn't have the nerve to go up and talk to anyone. That overnight bag made me feel ridiculous and square, so I didn't even finish my coffee before I got up and left.

The park was too cold to sit in, so I went back to

Myrna's place once more, but still no answer. There was nothing left to do, but to go back into the subway. At least, I could be warm down there, and it was cheap.

For a while it was all right. I kept changing trains, and every once in a while I'd try Myrna's number, getting more and more worried that maybe she'd gone away someplace. Still, I thought that if I could get through this night I'd figure something out by morning. I've always had this feeling: that if I could only get through the night, especially those awful nights when I couldn't go to sleep no matter what I did, everything bad would go away in the morning. Of course, it never did, but I still kept feeling that way.

That night, though, I couldn't keep my eyes open and I kept drowsing off in the subway. If only I could find a place to sleep, I thought, I'd be all right, but there was no place else to go. Those subway seats were hard as rocks, and I was worried someone would snatch my pocketbook or my suitcase, so I kept them on my lap, which was a pain.

I rode to all kinds of outlandish places: up to Van Cortlandt Park, down to Coney Island, up to Tremont Avenue in the Bronx, and out to Brighton. Places I had never heard of and certainly never wanted to see. I got along all right until around one or two in the morning I guess—by this time I'd given up all hope of Myrna getting home—and then I started worrying about the cops. There was one in every train, and I was torn between wanting to stick close to that nice safe-looking uniform and being afraid he would ask what I was doing and where I was going.

Nothing happened until someplace near the end of the line—out in Brooklyn, I think it was—a dreadful couple got on the train and started fighting. I mean real physical fighting. The man was one of those greasy guys with pointed boots and plastered-down hair, and the woman wore false eyelashes, which were crooked, and a hairpiece about a foot high. She looked sad, as if she had lost something she cared for and couldn't find it. They were both so drunk they could hardly walk, and the man hit her, calling her terrible, obscene names.

Then that awful woman turned to me, and said, "Did you see what he did? You look like a good, respectable kid. What do you think of a man who hits a woman? Let me tell you they're all alike, rotten everyone of them. Keep away from them, kid. Take my advice. . . ." Then she started to cry. "I've done everything in the world for this guy, everything, and look the way he treats me. . . ."

She sat down close to me and she smelled terrible. The man sat down opposite and was holding his head in his hands. I was afraid he was going to be sick. They were the saddest pair, and yet I felt they were hung up on each other, that they never could get along separately. They were lonely misfits, like me, except that they had each other. I wished I could do something for her, thinking that if all the misfits in the world could get together we could form our own kind of group, and the idea struck me that the hippies were doing just that, making a little world of their own, and I wanted desperately to join them instead of spending the night in the subway with a couple of drunks.

Then a cop came in from another car to see what all the woman's loud crying was about, and he made them show him their identification and tell him where they were going. They turned out to be married and going home, so he told them to cut out the disturbance or he'd take them in. Once the cop appeared they were all lovey-dovey with each other; they were really quite funny, although still sad, because I knew that the minute they got out of the subway they'd start fighting all over again.

When the policeman was finished with them he turned to me and asked why I was riding in the subway alone so late and where I was going. My heart was pounding furiously, but I quickly gave him a made-up name, which was partly my grandmother's, and a number on Mac-

Dougal Street, which wasn't Myrna's. He looked at me suspiciously and asked me if I had any identification with me, and I said no, that I hadn't, although I did have my driver's license in my bag. Still, I didn't think he'd have a right to ask to go through it. "If you're going to Mac-Dougal Street, you're on the wrong train," he said.

I didn't have to pretend to be flustered, because I was, and I said that I wasn't very familiar with the subway and I guess I'd gotten mixed up. "You sure did," he said, and he gave me careful directions on how to get off two stops later and cross over and take a train back to Manhattan. He stayed in that car until I got off.

By this time I was in a state, so I took a train back to Grand Central and went back to the ladies' room there. It was beginning to feel like home to me, and I wondered if I were going to spend all my time away from home in public bathrooms. I knew I couldn't stay there very long before the woman in charge would start asking me questions, so I washed my face and combed my hair and started out all over again.

Someplace along the line I picked up a paperback book, so now when a cop walked through the car I pretended I was reading, although I don't know one word of what I read that night. My next awful experience was when a bunch of rowdy boys came in, and I was terrified that they were going to attract the cops again. Then one of them got sick all over the floor, so I fled out of the car and left the train at the next station. Some of those stations were so cold and empty I nearly died shivering.

It was a big relief when around six in the morning men who were obviously workmen began coming into the subway. They were carrying their lunch boxes, going off to a day's work and they were the most welcome sight in the world. Dark Italians, Puerto Ricans, colored men and women, pink-cheeked Irishmen, they looked so solid and safe and real, I loved every one of them. I wondered what it would be like to have a father who went off with his lunch box every morning at six and a mother who stayed home and washed the clothes and did the cooking and ironing. It seemed kind of jolly to me, because I'd know where they were all the time and there wouldn't be a lot of phony parties and people and no one would expect me to be a great hit.

Just riding with those men and women, listening to them talk and laugh among themselves, made me feel better. I waited until seven to call Myrna again, and at last she answered the phone. What a relief! I had woken her up, and of course she was cross, because she'd been out terribly late, which I knew, but even so she told me to hurry up and get over to her place before she went to work.

For the first time I really paid attention to what train I was taking, and now, absolutely wide awake, I couldn't wait until I finally got to Astor Place. When I came out of the subway, it was bright and sunny and cold, but the wind had died down. It was one of those fabulously clear days. I walked across Washington Square Park singing. Getting through that night had been a fantastic accomplishment, and now I was truly on my way.

FOUR

"Yes, I'm sorry Claudia's not home tonight. I did so want you to meet her." Mrs. Nichols's mind was far from the coffee she was serving, and she hardly noticed when some spilled from the heavy silver pot in her hand. Nervously she wiped away the brown stain on the coffee table.

"We noticed the school all lighted up. Is there a dance?" Nancy McRoberts's intelligent, roving eyes were soaking up every detail of her boss's elegantly furnished room. Mrs. Nichols nodded, and Nancy continued in her low, cultivated voice. "She must have a wonderful time up here. The boys and girls I see around look so healthy and wholesome. I bet Claudia's very popular." Her voice implied that Mrs. Nichols's daughter would have to be.

"She has lots of friends. They do have a good time." Mrs. Nichols hoped she wasn't going to break down in tears. "I can't believe the talk we hear about the wild life in the suburbs. There may be a few rebellious young people, but not the ones we know. They all come from good families."

If she had to talk to the police, God forbid, that's what she would tell them. It was true. All of Claudia's friends came from good families, even if the boys wore their hair long.

Mrs. Nichols tried to keep up with the conversation, which was about the younger generation. Ordinarily it was a favorite topic, but her ear was tuned for the telephone. Surely Claudia wasn't going to carry this nonsense any farther and would call. Her feelings swung between frightened anxiety and resentment.

"I can understand rebellion," she heard herself saying. "We rebelled too when I was young, but these kids today seem to have no feeling *for* anything. They're against everything."

"I think they're for a new order," Mr. McRoberts said, "and I see no reason why we should expect them to provide the answers. A critic can say that a play's no good, but that doesn't mean he has to write a new third act."

"It's not the same thing." Mr. Nichols's preoccupied and bored expression was no comfort to his wife, but for once she was as eager as he for the evening to come to an end.

"But why do they need a new order? They have everything in the world. We didn't have anything when I was young. You young people don't know what the depression years were like." Mrs. Nichols wondered where Claudia had eaten her supper or if she had any supper. It was a cold night, and she hoped her daughter had dressed warmly. Perhaps she should buy her a real fur coat when she came home, one of those new, young furs, or perhaps she should be punished. It was hard to know what to do.

"Material things aren't going to solve the problem," Mr. McRoberts said.

"But nobody wants poverty." Nancy wrinkled her pretty nose to emphasize her point.

Mrs. Nichols suddenly remembered a story she'd read in the newspaper a few days earlier about two girls murdered in a lonely patch of woods in New Jersey. "Did they ever find the man who murdered those two girls?" she asked her husband abruptly.

His face turned a shade whiter. "No, they didn't, but they think one of the girls had a connection with him." His eyes were imploring her to stop thinking of such things.

"Kids are a lot safer here than they are in the city," Nancy was saying.

The conversation went on and on until Mrs. Nichols thought her head was going to burst with the pounding and the tension.

At last the McRoberts spoke about leaving, making an agonizingly slow departure, and Mr. and Mrs. Nichols were alone. "Oh, God, I thought they'd never leave. David, what shall we do?"

"I think the best thing to do right now is to get a good night's sleep. Claudia is probably having a wonderful time at some friend's house." He flicked the ashes off his cigar and loosened his tie. His anxious eyes did not reassure his wife.

"But what friend? I doubt if she's gone to anyone in Stony Point. Who else does she know?" Mrs. Nichols suddenly realized that outside of a few girls in Stony Point she had no idea who Claudia's friends were, or if she had any. "I'm going to try Edward again," she said determinedly. "Maybe he knows something."

This time Edward answered the phone. Mrs. Nichols told him what had happened and read him Claudia's note. "Have you any idea where she could be? Did she say anything to you?" Mrs. Nichols asked.

"I haven't the foggiest. But I wouldn't worry. You'll probably hear from her in a couple of days."

"But why would she do such a thing?" Mrs. Nichols didn't really expect an answer.

"Kids do crazy things these days. Have you called up any of her friends?"

"Not yet."

When Mrs. Nichols hung up the phone she turned to her husband again. "Do you think we should call up Cynthia or Ellen or Jane?"

"Not tonight. Let's wait until tomorrow morning. Then we'll see. Come on upstairs to bed."

Wearily Mrs. Nichols followed her husband up the stairs. But she didn't go into her own room; she went into Claudia's room instead. She had left the light on, and once again the quiet, orderliness of the room became frightening and oppressive. It's almost as if she were dead. . . . She pushed away the hideous thought, but the tears were rolling down her cheeks. The thought of the two murdered girls would not leave her. For reassurance she picked up Claudia's note and read it again; it was certainly Claudia's handwriting on the piece of paper.

The party dress still hanging on the closet door was ghostly. Quickly she opened the closet door to put it inside, and the first thing that caught her eye was Claudia's new coat hanging on its rack. In a panic she ran to her husband.

"She didn't even take her winter coat! David, something terrible has happened. I know it. Maybe she's been kidnapped. Either that or something awful is the matter with her. No girl in her right mind would go out tonight without a coat. Shouldn't we call the police?"

Mr. Nichols put his arms around his wife and tried to quiet her hysterical sobbing. He too read the note again. "I think we should give her a chance to call us. Please, darling, we must stay calm." His own face was white and drawn. "Hasn't she got more than one coat?"

Together they searched Claudia's closet, and then the hall closet downstairs. "I wish Anna had seen her go out." Mrs. Nichols's voice was desperate.

"Where's that old green coat she wears? I don't see it here." Mr. Nichols was going through the hall closet for the second time.

"That old coat? Why would she take that when she has a lovely new one? It doesn't seem right. Are you sure it isn't there?"

"Quite sure." Together they went back to Claudia's room, and they both studied the note once more.

"It's her handwriting," Mr. Nichols said. "People don't go around kidnapping sixteen-year-old girls. We're not that rich. Besides, why would she have cleaned up her room? No. She's left home for a few days. That's all there is to it. She'll be all right."

Mrs. Nichols sat down heavily on Claudia's bed. "You mean she's a runaway." She spoke the word painfully as she might have used the word *criminal.* "I just can't believe that this has happened to us. Why? We're good parents, we're intelligent. . . . I'd feel better if she'd taken a decent coat."

"Maybe she didn't think it was right to take it," Mr. Nichols said.

"Why?" Mrs. Nichols gave him a puzzled look. "You mean we give her too much? More than she wants to accept? Claudia loves clothes. All girls do."

Mr. Nichols raised his eyebrows questioningly. "I'm not so sure. You're always saying 'all girls,' " he said irritably. "They're not *all* alike."

"I never said they were." Her voice was irritable too. "I

suppose you'll tell me that I don't know my own daughter."

"It's possible," he said evenly. "I'm not blaming you. Maybe I've been a terrible father. I don't know. Or maybe it has nothing to do with us. I don't go along with all this Freudian business that the parents are to blame for everything. Come on, let's go to bed. I've got to get up early."

"So do I," she answered. As she did every other night, she went into her dressing room on one side of their large bedroom, while he went into his on the other. Mrs. Nichols felt a tremendous weariness as she took off her clothes, but automatically she hung up her kaftan in its place on the long rack of clothes. She stood staring, unseeing, at her dresses and suits, her many pairs of shoes neatly stacked on their metal racks, and wondered if her life with David might have been different if they hadn't lived in such a big house with so many places for them each to be alone. Would smaller space have kept them closer, more intimate?

She got into her twin bed, separated from his by two windows and a long, built-in set of cupboards and drawers (the room had looked so pretty and different that way), but she could not fall asleep. Her husband's familiar, rhythmic snoring was insistent. Had she forgotten, or had she never known, how to let him know when she needed to lie in his arms?

She heard the grandfather's clock in the downstairs hall strike two when she got out of bed and went back into Claudia's room. Bright moonlight etched out the small, familiar, precious possessions on the desk: a few stones picked up on the beach the previous summer, a quill pen that had been a Christmas present from Cynthia, a short, squat stone figure of a girl with a foolish face and long blond braids, chewed-up pencils, colored pens, and a large, unopened bottle of red ink. Mrs. Nichols stood in front of the desk irresolutely.

Then she turned away, knelt down next to the bed, and did something that she hadn't done since she'd been a small child. She folded her hands in prayer, and with her head bent against the bed she prayed fervently, asking God to take care of Claudia and to send her back to them quickly. "Please forgive me," she added in a low whisper, "if I've done anything wrong."

When she stood up Mrs. Nichols felt some relief, but she could not leave the room. She felt strongly that only there could she find some clue as to where Claudia had gone, and why. With a final shake of her head, she turned back to the desk. If she found something important, then she could decide later what to do with it. If she found nothing, no one need ever know that she had broken one of her favorite rules of advice to her readers: never invade your child's privacy. The words of one of her recent articles were clear in her memory: "Mothers who secretly read their son's or daughter's mail, or furtively sneak looks at a young person's diary, get what they deserve. Inevitably they discover things that are only painful, that they can do nothing about, things that are far better to leave locked up. You should always respect your child's privacy. . . ."

But this situation is different, Jean Nichols argued with herself. It could be a matter of life and death. She turned on the desk lamp and methodically started going through the drawers. It was cold in the room, even in her warm bathrobe, and she worked quickly, fearing that David might wake up and find her. She was sure he would not approve.

In the top drawer she found old report cards, class papers, some snapshots of Claudia's friends, hundreds of rubber bands and paper clips, old pencils, and, to her surprise, some pages of her own magazine articles. The other drawers turned up a few letters from Edward, a batch of old letters she and David had written to Claudia years ago at camp, and some letters from a boy Claudia had met at the beach the summer before. With a slight tremble of her hand, Mrs. Nichols started reading them. There were just a few, three or four, and they proved to be innocent, dull letters about the boy's school and hockey team.

In the bottom drawer she found a few sad, tattered souvenirs of parties, and a picture of herself holding the baby Claudia in her arms. The entire contents of the desk seemed to her so sad and so innocent that she wept again, longing to hold Claudia in her arms as she had in the snapshot, which she sat and stared at. The blandness of Claudia's personal accumulation added to the weight of her depression and was almost a disappointment. If she had found something significant, something that was revealing of the inner life of her daughter, her search would have been worthwhile. But the blankness that she encountered was uncomfortably close to the veiled, blank eyes that Claudia had so often turned upon her. In frustration and anger, Mrs. Nichols cried out, feeling that she had a stranger in the house, which was not what she had dreamed of when her baby daughter had been born.

Finally in a state of exhaustion, she went back to bed and fell into a deep and troubled sleep. At last the night was over. Both of the Nichols jumped when the alarm went off. "I thought it was the telephone for a minute,"

Mrs. Nichols said, sitting up in bed, while her husband turned the annoying buzzer off. He was out of bed, fumblingly collecting his clothes preparing to shower and get dressed.

"What are we going to do?" Mrs. Nichols demanded, as if she were continuing a conversation.

"I don't know. I can't think yet," her husband mumbled, and disappeared into the bathroom.

"I'm going to call Cynthia," Mrs. Nichols said to the closed door.

Impatiently she waited until a little after eight before making her call. After a preliminary greeting, ignoring the surprise in Cynthia's voice, she asked if she had seen or spoken to Claudia the day before.

"Yes, of course. I saw her at school, and then I spoke to her on the phone in the afternoon," Cynthia said. "Is she all right? I was sorry she didn't come to the dance."

"Did she tell you why she wouldn't go?"

"Not really. She said she didn't feel like it. Maybe she didn't want to go with Roger." Cynthia offered the suggestion tentatively.

"She won't be in school today. She went off to her grandmother's for a few days. We are worried about her, because she seems depressed, but I guess it's nothing important. I just thought she might have said something to you. Cynthia, if she should happen to call you, let us know, will you?"

"Yes, of course, Mrs. Nichols. I hope nothing's the matter."

"Why do you say that? Do you know of anything that's troubling Claudia?" Mrs. Nichols asked sharply.

"Oh, no, nothing special. But you know Claudia. She hates Stony Point and she has such high ideals. She's not an ordinary girl."

"No, of course not." Mrs. Nichols hung up the phone.

"What did Cynthia have to say?" Mr. Nichols asked.

"She said that Claudia hates Stony Point. Did you know that? And that Claudia has high ideals, as if there were some connection. It's all crazy! You'd think we were living in a ghetto. Claudia should have seen the tenement that I lived in. I never had a corner of my own, let alone a room, until I left home and earned my own living."

"Now don't get excited. I had hoped Cynthia would know something, but since she doesn't, I think we should go to the police," Mr. Nichols said.

The word police frightened Mrs. Nichols. "I told Cynthia that Claudia was with her grandmother for a few days."

"Why did you say that?"

Mrs. Nichols shook her head. "I don't know. It was the first thing that came into my head. I—I just couldn't say that we don't know where she is. It sounds so awful." She realized that she too had been clinging to the thought that Claudia had spent the night with a friend and they would hear from her first thing in the morning. Going to the police made Claudia's disappearance *real*.

"I'll have to call my office," she said in a tired voice.

"I will too."

Downstairs they sat through breakfast silently. "You tell Anna," Mrs. Nichols whispered.

"It would be better if you did."

"I can't. I can't talk about it. I can't believe it's really happened . . . not to us. . . ."

"Not saying anything won't make Claudia come back. Anna has to know. What if Claudia calls up while we're out?"

"I'll run upstairs and get the note and show it to Anna." When she came back her face was tearstained. "All Claudia's money is gone. Her Christmas money."

"I'm glad she can buy herself some breakfast," Mr. Nichols said grimly.

Mrs. Nichols went into the kitchen with Claudia's note, her voice breaking as she told Anna what had happened.

Anna was obviously shocked, but before she could say anything Mr. Nichols's voice interrupted them.

"Hurry up, Jean. Let's go."

"As soon as I call my office." She sat in front of the telephone several minutes before she picked up the receiver. All the appointments and daily harassments filled her mind, and they seemed like a haven. How wonderful to have nothing more to worry about than taking new pictures, writing her editorial for the next issue, selecting clothes for the fashion pages. . . . "I have some personal business I have to take care of today," she told her secretary. "I won't be in."

In the car, Mrs. Nichols broke the silence. "The police won't have to make a public announcement, will they?"

"I don't care if they shout it over every network. They should do whatever will help find her."

Mrs. Nichols sighed. His professional reputation wasn't at stake, but what would the millions of women who turned to her for advice think of a mother who couldn't keep her own daughter at home?

The bare, dilapidated police station was depressing in its coat of cream-colored paint, and young Captain Thompson was the brightest spot in it. He listened attentively to what Mr. and Mrs. Nichols had to say, and then discussed with them where their daughter might be.

"The chances are she's in New York. That's where the kids from around here go. Are there any relatives somewhere else she'd be apt to get in touch with?"

Mrs. Nichols shook her head. "I doubt it. The only possibility would be her brother, and we've spoken to him. He doesn't know a thing. What happens to these youngsters in New York? Do they get into trouble, I mean serious trouble?"

"Depends on the kid. Most of them want to be found by the end of a week and brought home. Some of them can't last out a day and a night. Did you bring any pictures with you?" He was eying them both shrewdly.

"No, we didn't. But I can get you some snapshots from last summer," Mr. Nichols said.

"Well, give me all the details." Captain Thompson took out a pad and started writing a description of Claudia, what she was wearing when she left, and when the Nicholses had discovered her departure. "Does she know anyone in New York?"

"My mother, her grandmother," Mrs. Nichols said. "But I doubt she'd get in touch with her."

"I'd check if I were you. You never know what these kids will do. Did you ask at the station if she was there yesterday?"

"No, we didn't. We haven't done anything," Mr. Nichols said. "We thought we'd give her a chance overnight to see if we'd hear from her." He showed the captain the note Claudia had left.

"I'll send out an alarm in this area and alert the special squad in New York. East Village, that's where a lot of them go. Is she a hippie? Take any drugs?"

"No," Mrs. Nichols said, shuddering. "She's a lovely, unsophisticated girl. She comes from a very good home. I simply can't imagine why she did such a thing."

"They're all lovely girls, according to their parents," Captain Thompson said coolly. "And they're all good homes until something like this happens. But we know more about the kids than the parents do."

"What do you mean by that?" Mrs. Nichols thought he was being impudent.

"We see the cars parked, and we see the pot parties. You'd be surprised."

Mrs. Nichols didn't like the way the captain was watching the effect of his words. She was beginning to take a great dislike to this unsympathetic young man. "I'm sure that you haven't seen my daughter," Mrs. Nichols said icily. "We're very worried that something terrible might have happened to her, and I hope you people know what you're doing."

"Ma'am, girls don't sit down and write notes when they

get mugged or kidnapped. I wouldn't worry too much if I were you."

"You're not me. I know my daughter, and I know a thing or two about young people myself. You and your staff had better take this seriously. We want to find our daughter."

The captain nodded courteously. "Don't worry, ma'am. We'll do our best."

Outside the police station Mrs. Nichols indulged in a tirade against stupid police officers who put everybody into one category and did not recognize that they were parents who cared.

"It's all part of the day's work for him," Mr. Nichols remarked. "I'm not sure it's a good idea to antagonize the police. We want their help."

Although her husband's comment left her completely frustrated, Mrs. Nichols didn't answer.

Together they drove to the railroad station, and leaving his wife in the car, Mr. Nichols went in to speak to the stationmaster. He came back with a discouraged face. "He can't remember. He says he was busy, and he thinks there was a girl who bought a one-way ticket to New York, but he's not sure it was Claudia. He doesn't want to say."

"What's the matter with these people? No one wants to

help." There was a desperate note in Mrs. Nichols's voice.

"He was nice enough. But he didn't want to commit himself, because he wasn't sure. Let's get those pictures back to Thompson, and then I guess I'd better get down to the office. Are you going in?"

Mrs. Nichols shook her head. "No, I couldn't bear to go in today. David, what are we going to do?"

"I'm afraid there's nothing we can do. We may as well give the police a chance to find her. You know that cop was right about the note. I'm convinced Claudia wants to be alone for a bit. There was a time, you know, when most girls in their teens packed off and left home for the cities. It was the thing to do, to find work in a factory. We're not used to their going anymore, but Claudia's not doing anything so new."

"I left home, but I didn't do it this way." Mrs. Nichols's eyes were unhappy. "And I had a terrible home. I *had* to get out. But Claudia, in the middle of her senior year of high school, doesn't have any reason. . . ."

After they left Claudia's pictures with the police, and Mrs. Nichols dropped her husband at the train station, she drove home slowly. The long hours of the day ahead were frightening, and alone in the car her usually composed face crumpled. A whole day away from her office loomed as endless time, and as she passed the neat, small cottages that lined the streets of the village, she wondered what all those other women were doing in their houses. How did they occupy themselves? What did they do after the men left for work and the children for school? Surely doing the breakfast dishes and making the beds didn't take long, and then what?

She tried to picture what their day would be like. Perhaps they spoke to their friends on the phone, or watched television, or baked pies, or cleaned up the bureau drawers. . . . Were they lonely, did they have friends? She wished that she knew some of the village women, feeling somehow that right now some plain, simple friend would be comforting. In her mind she went over the list of women she knew, practically all of them through her work, and there was not one that she wanted to talk to. I don't really have a close friend, she thought to herself.

She tried to shake off the depressing thought, reminding herself that she was known as the woman with a million friends. Just last night little Nancy McRoberts had said when they were leaving, "It was so nice of you to have us. I know you're so busy with so many people. You have so many friends."

Yes, there were lots of parties, lots of women in the office, endless luncheon dates, teas, cocktail meetings, men and women she wanted to keep up with. . . . There never was enough time to see all the people one wanted to and needed to. But real friends?

The house had an unnatural quietness. She went into the kitchen to find Anna, relieved that at least there was Anna, and Anna knew. "The police will send out a description," she reported, sitting down at the kitchen table. "Where do you think she is?"

"She's a good girl. She'll be all right. Here have a cup of coffee. It's good and hot."

"Does Claudia ever talk to you?" Mrs. Nichols wished she knew what Anna was thinking. *Another stranger in my house.* . . . Anna had worked for them for many years, but what did she know about her? Nothing except that she had come from Sweden a long time ago, that her husband was dead, and on her time off she went to New Jersey to visit her married sister and her nieces and nephews. With the right clothes and hairdo she would be quite handsome. Mrs. Nichols studied the tall, quiet, strong-boned woman who ran her house and wondered what she thought of them.

"No, Claudia doesn't talk much. She's always very polite to me, very nice, not sassy like some of the girls. She's a quiet girl."

"She didn't used to be, when she was younger. When she was small she used to talk a mile a minute. I wonder if she talks to anyone."

"She talks to her friends. I hear her on the phone. I don't listen to what she says, but I can hear her talking."

"I mean really talk, confide in them."

Mrs. Nichols walked around the kitchen restlessly, and then up to her room. The policeman had told her to call her mother, but she didn't want to. She could hear the disapproval in her mother's voice. Her mother would find some excuse to blame her. She would probably repeat again that mothers should stay home unless they needed the money. There had been a time when Jean Nichols had thought that her mother would be proud of her career, proud of how she had pulled herself out of the grimy, bleak poverty they had lived in, proud of the way she had made a name for herself without even a college degree. But soon after she had gotten married, when the children were small, and David was beginning to make a good living, her mother had nagged her to stop working. She and her mother had quarreled over the situation endlessly. Each time Jean had moved up to a bigger job, a bigger salary, she had been afraid to tell her mother, although she had never been able to resist either. Quite consciously she had taunted her mother with her successes: See what a success I am, you should be proud of me. . . .

But the response always had been her mother's cold look of disapproval, her questioning the price of the dress Jean was wearing, her remarking that her daughter's hair was too light. No, she was damned if she'd call her mother, and she would do everything possible to keep her mother from finding out about Claudia's disappearance. Mrs. Nichols wandered about the empty house restlessly, turning on the television and turning it off, picking up a magazine and not reading it. She didn't know what she would have done if Anna hadn't been there to talk to once in a while.

FIVE

Myrna's place was like great. A crazy skylight, two wild Siamese cats, and a beautiful, chaotic mess that made me feel free, the way I could never feel in a million years in my mother's house.

That's another thing about my mother. She has an insane fetish about emptying ashtrays (my father says one day she'll set fire to the house the way she doesn't wait for a cigarette to burn out—they both have a thing about fires), and she worships *neatness* as if it mattered whether every chair and pillow is exactly in its right place and every piece of clothing hung up in a closet. That woman is a slave to her possessions. You can't imagine the fuss she makes if an ordinary new frying pan comes into the house, how it has to be *seasoned* before anyone can use it, and a hundred times I've seen her straighten out the rugs and move a chair a quarter of an inch *before* she goes out of the house.

Neatness is one of our running battles, as if it's a crime to have clothes on a bed or a chair in a room where no one except me is going to see them, and I wouldn't care if the queen of England saw them anyway. What's the sense of hanging clothes up if I'm only going to take them out and wear them the next day? Things are only things, and if they get in the way they can be kicked under the bed. None of them are important, unless it's something absolutely beautiful like a fine drawing or painting or a lovely shell or stone, and even those can be dispensed with if necessary. What I mean is that things were invented to serve man, and not the other way around. Even my brother Edward carries on like a maniac if a shirt gets lost in the laundry, as if he couldn't go out and buy another. I couldn't believe what went on about the property when my parents bought their horrible house. I think there was some kind of an argument over who owned three feet or something ridiculous like that. They did nothing but talk about the boundary line for months, and my father was ready to go to court before it got straightened out. "You don't understand," they kept telling me, "we only want what's coming to us," but they didn't understand that none of the fight was worth all the talk and arguing and discussion that they wasted on it. Respect for private property! I think that if there were no fences and people could walk any place they pleased the world would be a lot nicer.

"You look awful," Myrna said to me. She looked pretty sad herself with black lines under her eyes, but of course I knew she'd been out all night, and neither one of us was stupid enough to ask questions.

"I've been riding in the subway all night. It was kind of fun in a sick sort of way. Right now all I want is a bed and some sleep."

"The bed's in the other room. Just throw the junk off it. I've got to go to work. You got any money?"

"Sure, lots."

"Can you lend me two bucks? I get paid today, and I'll give it back to you tonight."

By the time Myrna left she looked terrific. She's a great looking girl, kind of Mexican or Spanish, and she wears way-out clothes that look marvelous on her. That day she had on some kind of orangey and pink thing and long black earrings, and then she covered herself up with a wild fur coat that she said she'd bought for eight dollars.

"Where do you work?"

"In a mannequin shop. We're making Santa Clauses now for next year, and that damn angel hair we paste on gets into everything. I've got it in my nails, my skin, everywhere. I'll be glad when we're finished with this job See you later."

About a minute after she left I was asleep.

I was awakened by a tremendous crash, a great clash of pots that the cats must have knocked over, but I didn't go look because I didn't care. Then the phone rang, and it took me forever to find it behind a pile of books, and it was Myrna telling me it was almost four o'clock. Her boyfriend Hugh would be coming in, and he had a key, so I shouldn't be scared if a strange man with a red beard walked into the apartment, because that was Hugh. She also said that if I went out I could buy a box of spaghetti and a can of tomato paste, but I told her I wasn't going out, and she said it didn't matter, that she'd stop on her way home.

The apartment was really crazy. Behind the living

room and the tiny bedroom was the room with the skylight, which was a combination bathroom and kitchen.
There was no shower and the bathtub had a lot of dirty
dishes in it. I took them out and gave myself a kind of
sponge bath, wondering what would happen if Hugh
walked in, but he didn't. When I was dressed again I was
starving, and I found some cheese crackers, so I sat down
with the box of crackers to watch the cats. They were
absolutely beautiful. Myrna had a high bookcase, and the
two of them sat up on the top shelf and stared at me with
their blue eyes. Then suddenly without any warning one
jumped across to a table and the other chased it, and
those two crazy cats chased each other around the room
until they both went back to the bookcase, rested a few
minutes, and then started all over again.

Watching those cats was the most interesting thing I'd
done in months. I didn't think about anything. I was absolutely happy sitting there, eating those cheese crackers
and watching those two cats. They were so beautiful and
sure of themselves, I kept waiting for one of them to miss
the table or the bookcase, but they never did. I didn't try
to go near them or pet them, because I knew they wanted
to be left alone the same as I did. It was beautiful in that
room watching those cats.

Then Hugh came in, and he sure enough had a red

beard, and red hair, and he was nice because he didn't say anything. He just kicked some stuff off a chair and sat down and watched the cats with me. After a little while he put on some records, and the music got the cats even more excited. Both of us sat there laughing at them.

When Myrna came home Hugh cooked a pot of spaghetti and we had a great meal and I was fine until the telephone rang. Then I jumped, and said, "I hope it isn't my family."

Myrna stared at me. "Did you tell them you were coming here?"

"No, of course not. But they're pretty sneaky, and maybe they figured it out."

"What do you want me to tell them?" The phone was ringing all the while.

"Tell them she jumped into the river," Hugh said.

That made me laugh. "No, you'd better not. Just say you haven't heard from me in ages."

Of course, it wasn't my family at all, but someone telling Myrna about a party at Bob's apartment over on East Ninth Street, and she said we'd be over later. Then she asked me something odd. "Do you want your family to find you?"

"What makes you ask that?"

Hugh laughed. He had a loud, slightly hysterical laugh, as if he thought the whole world were crazy, which he undoubtedly did. "She's the friendly village witch doctor. Be careful or she'll start analyzing you."

"I don't mind. But why did you ask, Myrna?"

"I wanted to know. If you want them to find you, you play it one way. If you don't, you play it another."

"Well, I don't. Although I suppose sometime I'll get in touch with them. Maybe when I'm an old lady." I didn't mean that last remark, because I'm not mean or cruel, and I figured that sooner or later I'd drop them a line. Frankly I wondered if they'd mind my leaving very much. I knew my mother would be disappointed that I hadn't turned out the way she'd hoped I would—being popular and going to college and all—but since I was the way I am, I thought she might be relieved to have me out of the house. God knows she'd told me often enough how much it pained her to see me moody and morose, how my sloppiness and carelessness upset her, how much it cost them to bring me up, and how hard they both worked to give Edward and me the best of everything. So who could blame me for thinking she'd be pleased to be rid of me?

"You'd better steer clear of the cops," Myrna said.

The idea that the police might be looking for me came

as a surprise. "I'm certainly not going to stay cooped up here." I was already beginning to feel restless, eager to move around, to see what was going on.

"No, but if you don't want to get picked up, you'd better be careful. Get some dark glasses and do something different with your hair. Pin it up. I'll lend you a hat to stick it under, and you can buy a fur coat for a few bucks."

My new life began to sound exciting, like a Hitchcock movie.

Myrna gave me a wild black velvet hat with a wide, floppy brim, and that night she had me wear her fur coat, because she said that old green thing of mine would be spotted in a minute if anyone were looking for me.

We walked over to East Ninth Street, and up a lot of stairs in a smelly tenement, to Bob's apartment. I could smell the pot out in the hall and hear the music.

Inside there was this kind of old, at least thirty-five, black man with his head draped in an African turban, sitting in the middle of the room playing a drum, and a couple of girls squatting on the floor beside him playing guitars. They were playing real low, and the music was good. There were no chairs in the room, and hardly any light, and everyone was on the floor or on pillows. I guess they were hippies, because they all had long hair, the boys and the girls, and wore lots of jewelry—earrings and beads, necklaces and rings. It's hard to describe the clothes they wore, because no two of them looked alike. The colors were wild—purples and oranges, reds, yellows, and vivid blues—and there were lots of full skirts and tight pants, satin and velvet and leather waistcoats, crazy prints. They looked beautiful lounging on the floor listening to the music and smoking.

Myrna asked me if I'd ever smoked before, and I told her the truth that I had twice, up at Stony Point. It didn't do anything for me so I wasn't excited about it, but I took a deep puff of the reefer they offered me anyhow. The stick went around the room with each person taking a puff, like a ceremonial, something like a group of Indians smoking a peace pipe. And it was peaceful. Of course, I'd never discussed marijuana with my parents, but I'd heard them talk about it enough, and I used to laugh to myself at how excited they got about kids taking dope when everyone knew that the cigarettes they smoked and the alcohol they drank was infinitely worse. Besides most kids don't smoke often; it's too expensive. They try it once or twice to see what it's like. As for the pills and the hard stuff, I think that's pretty sick, and I wouldn't touch any of it if you begged me. I mean, who wants to get stuck on something that keeps you from knowing what's happening, makes you loony, or gives you deformed babies. Any-one has to be out of his mind to experiment with that stuff.

That night I smoked along with everyone else, and as I said it didn't really do anything for me, except I heard more notes of the music than I'd ever heard before, and if I closed my eyes halfway I could see all kinds of wonder-ful shapes and colors. Also, I got terribly hungry, but there were only potato chips to eat, so I stuffed myself with them. I wasn't paying any attention to anyone, just feeling glad that I was there and not home in my room at Stony Point. I got to thinking about my room and what a terrible square place it was. I never had bothered to fix it up with anything, I guess because I knew it was hopeless with the dreary maple furniture my mother had put into it—early American she called it, but it looked like early deadville to me. The things I might have wanted my mother would have hated, and there'd only have been another row. But if I ever got around to having a pad of my own, I was thinking, I'd make it look great. When I closed my eyes I could see all kinds of wonderful rooms, big rooms with very little in them: lots of pillows, a few divans, and marvelous decorations on the walls. . . .

"Say, kid, can you move over? You're jamming your elbow into my ribs." I was still tired from the night before, and I guess I'd half fallen asleep against this boy next to me.

"I'm sorry," I mumbled.

He was peering at me from out of dark eyes under bushy eyebrows. "What are you doing here anyway? You look about fourteen." He had turned around and was leaning on his elbow to see me better.

"I'm not. I'm eighteen," I told him.

"The hell you are. But it doesn't matter. I don't care."

"You're right. It's none of your business."

I tried to go back to my half dreams, but I couldn't. And the strangest thing happened. There I'd been lying right next to him, not even aware that he existed, and then when we weren't touching at all I could think of nothing except the feeling of his physical presence about six inches away from me. It was weird and irritating. Without saying a word he intruded upon me, making me conscious of his breathing, of the graceful way he was stretched out, with his arms folded under his head, flat on his back staring up at the ceiling. I was afraid to look at him, afraid he'd somehow snoop out how terribly conscious I was of his body, of his being there next to me.

I didn't know what to do. I couldn't think of anything to say, and I didn't think he felt like talking anyway. I was afraid to move for fear I'd bump into him again, so I

stayed in one position until I got such a cramp in my leg I
had to shake it.

"What the hell are you doing?"

"I've got a cramp in my leg. I'm sorry, but shaking it is
the only thing that helps."

"Oh, for Christ sake. Here, let me rub it. You're shaking
the whole floor." He took hold of my leg and rubbed it so
hard I thought he'd rub right through my tights.

"It's all right now."

"When did you eat last?" He was watching me take
another handful of potato chips.

"I had supper tonight, but I'm hungry."

"So am I. Come on out, infant, and I'll buy you a hamburger. You don't belong here anyway."

"I'm not an infant, and I don't belong anywhere. But
okay on the hamburger," I added quickly.

When he stood up he looked like a big shaggy dog with
his dark beard and a heavy sweater and shoulders ten feet
wide. He laughed when I put on the velvet hat and the
fur coat. "Looks like you're dressed up for Halloween."

If I hadn't been so hungry I would have told him to get
lost.

In the hamburger joint he said his name was Steve, and
that he'd left college because he got tired of looking at
the fishbowl. "It was great for a while, you know, to

watch the fish. They had fights and they made love and some of them ate up their babies. But after three months it got boring. They kept doing the same things all the time."

"Cats are better." I told him about watching Myrna's cats. "They do the same thing, but they do it differently."

"But you can't have fish or a bird if you have cats. I had a raccoon once. He was the greatest. I had him for a whole summer. Then my father shot him, because he bit my kid brother's finger. I buried him in the woods."

"Did you cry?"

"Of course, I cried."

"Why didn't your father let him go free?"

"Because he's a bastard."

Then we went back to talking about cats. We talked about a lot of things. It was a beautiful conversation, because he didn't ask me anything and I didn't ask him. This time when we got up to leave he didn't laugh at Myrna's coat, although I told him it was hers.

"You're a beautiful girl," he said to me.

"Don't put me on. You'll spoil everything."

"I usually do," he said. "But I'm not putting you on. I think you're beautiful."

Already I had started watching for his smile, because it was gentle and sweet, not at all the way he talked. Some of his talk, though, was sweet too, especially when he described the different animals, like five baby deer mice, he'd raised.

I looked at him to see if he really meant what he said, and I decided he did. It was the first time anyone had ever told me straight out that I was beautiful, and it made me all quivery and trembly, but I wasn't embarrassed because Steve was the kind of person who didn't embarrass you by anything he said. He didn't go out of his way to impress or shock me, but still I was impressed when he said that in order to make a beautiful new world everything had to be destroyed first. "It's not a new idea," he added. "The Nihilists believed the same thing over a hundred years ago. Too bad they never got around to doing it."

"You mean kill everybody?"

"Not people. Outworn ideas, customs, prejudices. Destroy this society and start all over again."

"But they never let you. It's impossible. Sometimes I tried to do that at home. I'd make up my mind that everything was going to be different. A clean slate. My mother and father were strangers. We'd just met and I was visiting them. Forget all the old hang ups. I thought that if I could think of them differently, things would change. But it never worked. I'd listen to one of their conversations, trying to be interested and polite, and in a few minutes I'd get all the same old feelings back."

"You can't do it that way by pretending. That's what white people do about blacks, pretend they're thinking differently, but their reactions are the same. You have to knock down the structure from the bottom up. Change who's in control. Black power is one way."

We were walking across the park, the wind in my face, and Steve took off my hat because he said he liked to see my hair blow. "The hat's supposed to be a disguise."

"What for?"

"My parents may have the cops out looking for me."

"You think they would?"

"I suppose so."

"I haven't heard from my parents in four months."

"You said your father was a bastard."

"Yeah, he is."

I tried to picture Steve's father holding a gun in his hand and shooting the raccoon, and Steve as a little boy watching, and then turning away his face when the gun went off. I wondered if his kid brother had been there too, and where his mother was. I saw a row of grinning faces dancing around a dead raccoon. I put my arm through Steve's, and we went on walking.

Myrna had given me a key, and I said good-bye to

Steve downstairs. I didn't want Steve to come up with me in case Myrna and Hugh were there. I wanted to keep Steve to myself. He didn't say anything about seeing me again, and I felt terribly lonely when he walked away. I watched him, a big shaggy bear, go down the block and turn the corner. He didn't look back once to wave or anything.

I knew Myrna was home, because the lights were on and the cats were eating. My suitcase was on top of the table. The door to the bedroom was closed, and I knew Hugh was there too, because I could hear them talking low. I didn't know what to do. I got up my courage and knocked on the door once very lightly, but they didn't answer. I guess if they heard me they thought I was one of the cats.

I sat there thinking about Steve, which made me feel terribly sad, because he had walked away as if he had a place to go, and I knew that if Steve were connected with someone he was truly connected. Besides, why would he bother with me, a skinny kid who couldn't even keep Roger Ferris interested?

Finally I got undressed, but I wanted to clean my teeth and wash my face and go to the bathroom. The bedroom was quiet now, and I didn't dare knock on the door again. I walked up to it a few times and thought I'd knock sharply. I mean, after all, I had a right to go to the bathroom, but I couldn't do it, even though I felt foolish. I wondered if people's bladders broke, and if they died from not going to the bathroom, and whether I could last through the night.

The cats were staring at me, and I knew they thought I was pretty stupid, so I dumped everything off the broken-down sofa, covered myself with Myrna's coat, and turned out the lights, although the street lamp shining in made the room look just about the same. Then I started to giggle, because I'd spent most of last night in bathrooms—thinking of all those rows of toilets made me feel worse, of course—and now tonight I couldn't get near one. I remembered smoking my first cigarette in Cynthia's bathroom when I was thirteen, and I wondered if the story of my life was going to be the joys and sorrows of bathrooms. Perhaps when I got old I'd fall in a bathtub and die. If I didn't die that night.

SIX

The odor of stale water and dead flowers pervaded the room. Automatically Mrs. Nichols got up from the sofa and started for the kitchen with two bowls in her hands.

"Why are you doing that now? I thought we were going to have a discussion." Mr. Nichols gave the last word a foreboding emphasis.

"Yes, Mother. For heaven's sake don't start fussing with

that stuff now." Edward's sulky face glowered at his mother.

"We don't have to have dead flowers in the house, do we?"

"What's the difference?" Mr. Nichols looked to his mother-in-law Mrs. Kinney for support, but she was sitting with hands folded and lips tightly compressed, unyielding. Deliberately Jean Nichols, carrying the bowls as if they were sacred offerings to the gods, went on her way to the kitchen.

"Dear God," she addressed Anna, "if only my mother hadn't insisted on coming up this weekend. I didn't want her to know about Claudia."

"Yes, Mrs. Nichols." Anna's serene face was noncommittal.

"She'll get herself in a state. She's such a worrier, although there's not a line in her face. But having her here now is almost too much. . . ." She dumped the dead flowers into the wastebasket. Her mother's arrival was the last straw in a harrowing week. Even without the awful worry about Claudia, the endless arguments with Mrs. Kinney caused enough tears. Mrs. Nichols could not forgive her mother for her insistence on living so far out in Brooklyn that a taxi ride cost five dollars. Why, when the Nichols were paying the rent and wanted her to be in Manhattan? In turn, Mrs. Kinney badgered her daughter for wasting money, buying her a color TV set for Christmas, when Mrs. Kinney liked black and white better.

Jean Nichols put her hand to her head in despair. Too much to cope with.

"Jean, Jean. Hurry up. That police officer will be here in a little while."

"All right, all right." She must hang on to her control.

"I don't understand you people," Mrs. Kinney was saying. "You've been sitting here doing nothing for days, and God knows what's happened to that child. Two educated, intelligent people. If you had called me right away. . . ."

"And what would you have done?" Jean Nichols faced her mother.

"I'd rip the city apart. I'd go on television. I'd advertise in the newspapers. I'd get after them at police headquarters. A person doesn't just disappear. . . ."

"There are thousands of missing persons every year," Mr. Nichols said wearily, "that the police can't find. And we haven't just been sitting here doing nothing. The police have been searching for her. New York's a big city to find someone in, if she's in New York."

"I'm sure she's in New York," Edward said. "That's where all the kids go."

"Well, I don't understand it. My children were brought up in a cold-water tenement flat, but they never ran away from home. They didn't have all the fancy things your children have. . . ." Mrs. Kinney had a talent for leaving her sentences meaningfully unfinished.

"We got out as fast as we could. Don't kid yourself."

"All these recriminations are getting us nowhere. The whole purpose of our getting together is to decide what the next step should be." Mr. Nichols spoke in his lawyer's voice.

"Can we hurry it up? I've got to get back to school. I've got a paper to write that's due tomorrow."

"As always I suppose you left it till the last minute," Mrs. Nichols said to her son. "It's your little sister, Edward. You've always adored her, and she worships you."

"She didn't run away from me. She ran away from you two. It may be the smartest thing she ever did."

"And what do you mean by that? What a cruel, unfeeling thing to say. Is this such a bad home for you? You don't seem to be suffering with four thousand dollars a year for your college and a car of your own."

"Jean, for God's sake, stop it. I've been thinking we should hire a private detective. The police have hundreds of cases, but our own agency could concentrate on Claudia."

"That sounds like a good idea," Mrs. Nichols said. "Is it terribly expensive?"

"I don't give a damn about the expense. The trouble is, though, I don't want the police to stop whatever they're doing, because we have someone of our own on the case."

"Do you have to tell them?" Edward asked.

"It would be ethical."

"I told you what I would do," Mrs. Kinney said. "I saw a woman on television whose little boy was lost. She made such a beautiful appeal it nearly broke my heart. The boy scouts and the fire department, they all went out to look for him. You should have seen the mother. . . ."

"Did they find him?" Edward asked.

"Yes, poor thing. He was drowned in a pond. Their only boy, such a terrible thing to happen. . . ."

"That was in a small town, Mother," Mrs. Nichols said. "I don't think it would do much good in New York. Besides, Claudia hardly ever watches television, and she never reads a newspaper."

"What kind of a girl are you bringing up? These days not to watch television or to read a newspaper." Mrs. Kinney sniffed.

They were interrupted by Anna saying that the police officer had arrived.

Mr. Nichols promptly offered Captain Thompson a

drink, which he refused saying that he never drank while on duty. To their anxious eyes and questions he shook his head. "We haven't come up with a thing so far. Sorry. But it's not unusual. If these kids don't want to be picked up, they learn the ropes pretty fast. Have you questioned all her friends? There must be someone that she knows in the city." He turned to Edward. "How about you? Don't you know anyone your sister might be staying with?"

"I'm afraid not. We went our own ways pretty much."

"Tell me some more about the girl. What kind of things does she like to do?" He looked from one to the other. "We have her pictures, but we really don't know very much about her."

"I've told you that our daughter is a lovely, normal girl. She does the same things that every girl does. She likes parties, she's a good dancer, she loves music, she's a good student, and she likes sports. In the winter she skates, and in the summers she goes swimming. What more do you want to know?" Mrs. Nichols's nervous impatience did not disturb the young captain.

"If you'll excuse my saying so, ma'am, the kind of girl you describe doesn't pick up and leave home. They always have a problem. What about a boyfriend? You haven't mentioned anyone." He accepted the cigarette Edward offered him.

"She had lots of boyfriends," Mrs. Nichols said. "We don't believe that girls her age should go with only one boy."

Mr. Nichols raised his eyebrows. "As a matter of fact, she didn't go out with boys very much. She's a quiet girl. Liked to stay in her room and play records and read."

"Not in any neurotic way," Mrs. Nichols cut in. "I'm telling you my daughter is a normal, healthy girl."

"Except that she's an oddball," Edward said gently. "She's just not with it, that's all."

"What do you mean?" Captain Thompson's face brightened.

Mrs. Kinney leaned forward in her chair. "She once told me that she hated clothes. That she could happily wear only a pair of shorts and an old shirt. That's not a normal, healthy girl for you."

"How ridiculous! Look at her closet. It's full of pretty dresses." Mrs. Nichols lighted a cigarette.

"That she never wore," Mr. Nichols murmured.

"I want to know what you mean when you say that she's an oddball." Captain Thompson turned to Edward deliberately.

"It's hard to explain. She's not like the girls I know at school. She has crazy ideas. One time she wanted to go to India and live in a leper colony. She was mad at me, because I accepted a car from my folks. You know, crazy things like that. She said we had too much and other people had too little, as if our doing without would help."

"You mean hippie ideas?"

Edward shrugged, "You got me. I don't dig those hippies at all. They're a bunch of nuts who don't know what they want as far as I can make out."

"She never talked about things like that with us." Mr. Nichols spoke quietly, his face worried.

"My daughter a hippie, taking dope!" Mrs. Nichols paled. "I don't believe it."

"It's a possibility," Captain Thompson said calmly. He stood up. "I think I get the picture now," he said genially. "I'll pass this information on to our New York special squad. I think it will help."

"We're considering hiring a private detective agency," Mr. Nichols said. "That wouldn't interfere with you people, I'm sure, would it?"

Captain Thompson smiled. "It's your money, sir. Before I did that, I'd go down to New York, below Fourteenth Street, and get around to all the spots myself. Especially Greenwich Village and the East Village. I have a hunch that's where you'll find her."

"We wouldn't know where to begin to go," Mrs. Nichols said. The suggestion was frightening . . . to look for Claudia and perhaps find her with some dirty, long-haired beatniks. . . .

"Perhaps your son could help you." Captain Thompson's smile turned into a grin.

"I have to get back to school," Edward mumbled.

"He's a nice young man," Mrs. Kinney said, when the door closed behind the policeman.

"I don't like him at all. He keeps looking at me as if I don't know my own daughter, and he's too young." Mrs. Nichols nervously put out one cigarette and fixed another into her long, amber holder. "We're no further than we were before."

"I think his suggestion that we go cruising around ourselves is a good one. I wish you could come with us, Edward."

Edward shook his head. "I can't right now, Dad. Maybe next week. But you and Mom'll have no trouble. Just go in and out all the streets, into the coffee houses and night spots."

"It seems like a wild-goose chase to me. Even if that's where she is, we could keep missing her."

"Of course, it's no guarantee, Jean. But at least we'd be doing *something*. Anything is better than waiting."

"I'll go," Mrs. Kinney said. "I'll walk until I find her."

"No, Mother. Not with your hip. I'd just as soon we didn't have to send you to the hospital again."

"I can walk as good as anyone. Better than you in those high heels." Mrs. Kinney made a sound that resembled a snort. "Bet you paid forty dollars for those nothing shoes. I don't know how you wear them in this cold weather."

"Mom takes taxis. She never walks."

The telephone rang, and Mrs. Nichols jumped to answer it. When she came back to them her face was excited. "It was Cynthia. She said she thought of some place where Claudia might be. There is a Stony Point girl who went to the high school, Myrna Lowe, who has an apartment in the Village. Cynthia thinks Claudia might be there. I'm going to call her up right away."

"No, wait a minute. Don't be in such a hurry. I don't think we should call. I think we should get in the car and go down there. If Claudia doesn't want to see us, this Myrna girl can say she isn't there, and Claudia can leave."

"That makes sense, Dad."

"Do you really believe that Claudia wouldn't want to see us?" Mrs. Nichols's voice was shocked.

"She said in her note that she wanted to be left alone, didn't she? My God, Jean, stop living in some fantasy dream world about your daughter. She's an unhappy kid and for whatever reason she holds it against us. We're not the happy family you write about in your magazine. This is for real."

"Please don't shout at me."

"I'm sorry. We're all in a nervous state. Come on, let's get going."

SEVEN

This place is wild. I moved into a crash pad, because I couldn't stand being with Myrna and Hugh, and besides I didn't think they wanted me although they didn't say so. Hugh dropped hints saying that I wasn't getting anywhere with them, not learning about life or what my own thing was (whatever that might be), and that I was using Myrna and himself as a mother and father image. That really made me laugh. If he ever saw my mother and father, he'd know how far off he was. He could have said just as well that the cats were a mother and father image, because they were as much like my parents as he and Myrna. The truth, which I didn't mention, was that I was using their place (or pad, which he liked to call it and which I found a great affectation because I knew he didn't use the word naturally) because I needed a place to sleep and to get washed in.

There were eight of us sleeping in a room over on Avenue B and for three mornings in a row the girl next to me woke up crying. Finally she said it was her birthday, and she was fourteen years old. She was crying because no one kissed her good morning and said happy birthday, and at home she always had a cake. I told her that I'd go out and buy her a cake, but that only made her cry all the harder. Then Timo, who was some kind of a leader, said he'd take her over to the fifth precinct and turn her in so the cops could call her parents. She said that she didn't want to go, but I noticed that she jumped right up and for the first time since I'd seen her she combed her hair and asked him how soon he wanted to leave.

It seemed odd to me that anyone would be crying for a birthday cake, because I remembered how corny I thought my mother was when she brought me a big fancy

cake with my name written all over it from some ritzy
Madison Avenue shop for my sixteenth birthday. But
maybe when I was fourteen it was different. I don't remember that far back. But I guess it doesn't make any
difference whether you're crying because you get a cake
or you don't, the point being that whatever it is you want
or you don't want, parents don't hear anything you say,
and they wouldn't understand it if they did. They walk
around with cotton in their ears and a mirror in front of
them looking only at their own image.

The other thing that hung me up at Myrna's was her
brother. Those two really liked each other. They always
were lending each other money, and Danny sometimes
came and cleaned up the place and went shopping for
her, because she was working and he wasn't, and she fed
him and took him to parties. When they were together
they talked about everything under the sun and made
everyone else, even Hugh, feel excluded. If I had had a
brother like Danny, maybe I never would have left home.
But Edward betrayed me, and I'll never forgive him.

There was a time when I adored Edward. He was
really a hero to me. A million years ago, when I was seven
or eight, my father gave me a spanking (which was itself
unusual so I must have done something terrible), and I
was screaming bloody murder. Edward, who was all of

around twelve, stalked up to him, and said, "Don't you hit her. I'll punch you if you hit her anymore."

My father laughed, and said, "Okay, Edward. But I wasn't really hurting her." Which wasn't true, because he was, but the thing is that he stopped. I followed Edward around afterward like a shadow, and I would have done anything in the world for him.

Until the time he betrayed me. I was twelve, and my parents were in New York overnight, and Edward was supposed to stay home with me. I don't remember where Anna was, but she wasn't home. I liked the idea of Edward and me being alone, and I cooked a great dinner for us: hamburgers and potato chips and ice cream and chocolate cake. It was like a private party for just the two of us. I remember it all exactly. But right after supper Edward said he was going out. My heart sank. It had been an unusually hot day in early June, the dark clouds were already gathering, and I knew we were going to have a thunderstorm. That year I was terrified of thunderstorms, and I thought that if we played Monopoly I wouldn't worry so much about the storm. Besides, with Edward I would be less scared than with anyone else.

"You'll be all right here," he said, "Nothing'll happen to you."

"But it's going to storm. You know I don't like thunderstorms." I couldn't tell him how frightened I was.

"Don't be stupid. You're perfectly safe in the house."

"But I'm scared. You said you'd stay home."

"Well, I'm not going to. And if you dare say anything, I'll kill you." He looked at me as if he meant what he said.

Then I started to cry. "If you go out, I'll never speak to you again." All my pride was gone.

"That'll suit me fine. You're the worst baby I ever saw in my life." The door slammed behind him. He had just gotten his driving license, and I could hear him taking the car out of the garage. I went to the window to watch him go, but the lightning had started already, so I ran away. If I get struck and the house burns down, he'll be sorry. . . .

The storm broke like all hell let loose. I'd never heard such loud thunder in my life, and the lightning crackled all over the sky. The first thing that happened was that sparks came out of the outlet where the toaster was attached, and I was too frightened to pull it out. Then all the lights went out, and I was alone in the pitch-black house. I was hoping that my parents would phone, I just wanted to hear someone's voice, but they didn't. Then the telephone wires got struck, and the telephone bell kept ringing wildly. I picked up the receiver once, scared of it, but there was only a lot of noise and crackling, so I put it down in a hurry.

I got into bed, put the pillows over my head, and lay there trembling, hating Edward. I knew then that everything was over between us. I knew that he didn't care about me at all, and that he understood nothing. He had grown up to be a selfish, self-centered, cruel person, nothing at all like the storybook brothers who had secrets with their sisters and lined up with them against the grown-ups. He had gone over to the other side and was leading his own excluding, private, nasty grown-up life; he had left me behind, alone. The door was slammed in my face forever, and I never would knock on it again.

Of course, I didn't say anything to my parents, and I went on as if nothing had happened, but I didn't trust Edward anymore. Now seeing Danny and Myrna together was too much, because they had what I used to think Edward and I would grow up to have.

Myrna couldn't understand why I didn't get in touch with my brother. She asked me about him a few times, but all I told her was that he wasn't the type. There were times, though, when I went into a telephone booth all ready to call him. Once I even dialed his number, but there was no answer, which was an omen. Typically he wasn't there when I needed him. I knew way deep down that it was no use trying to talk to him.

But believe me there were times when I thought I'd die if I didn't have a friend. The pad itself was awful with cockroaches, peeling paint, and, according to one girl, rats. Someone said that a rat bite could kill you, which seemed like a humiliating way to die.

Everyone told me I'd come at the wrong time, that the summer was much better. For one thing it wouldn't have been so beastly cold, and there would have been a lot more doing. The whole place was crazy with people sleeping at all hours, and fights starting up over nothing at all. One night someone dropped a beer can out the window, and it hit a Puerto Rican boy. He came tearing upstairs yelling about the dirty hippies, so the boys took out their chains, and God knows what would have happened if Timo hadn't been there. He stopped them saying it was stupid to use chains because someone had been hit by a beer can, and he told the Puerto Rican kid he was sorry and sent him away.

The kid left, although he turned at the door and spit on the floor with a face full of hate. I couldn't believe the expression on his face, but then I didn't know anything about the Lower East Side. I was only learning about the East Village, which was a tiny part of it. Outside there was a whole other world, where ordinary poor people lived: Puerto Ricans and Negroes, Jews and Irish, Italians and Polish. Terrific people, but they had lots of fights and most of them hated the kids.

There were always fights. Take this big black boy Gordon, for instance. He was beautiful, long and thin, and he always wore a marvelous serape over his turtlenecked sweater with lots of necklaces. But he hated the whites, and when he spoke he always seemed to be making a speech about whitey. "The time has come for revenge," he said. "Black power is not for thievery and murder, but it is impossible to live in America without becoming a thief and a murderer. Black power seeks to destroy what now is. What is happening here is only the same as what is happening in Asia, Africa, and Latin America. Black power is not antiwhite, it is against oppression, and if the whites are on the side of the oppressors, then we are forced to be antiwhite. . . ."

He had a beautiful voice, and when he spoke he really tore me up. But then there were other kids who used filthy words like *nigger* and said he was a menace, and once they tried to beat him up and nearly killed him.

I had to get out of that place, because although I could get free food there it was too confusing. I didn't know what was going to happen from one minute to the next, with kids going off on trips, and no one really loving anyone else. All the time I was hoping to run into Steve, but I didn't see him anywhere.

Also, there was the problem of money. When my mother wasn't talking about sex, she'd go off on the money bit, how we kids didn't understand the value of money, and how we should have grown up in the depression to know what a dollar meant. Of course, she was right, because I didn't know the first thing about money, although she was no example the way she threw it around so uselessly. But now I truly had to keep track of what I had, and it was unbelievable the way fifty dollars dwindled even though I bought only the barest necessities. I resisted buying hamburgers and sodas, which was hard, because the skimpy food at the pad was boring, and I began dreaming about the meals that Anna cooked at home. One thing I'll say about our house, the food was good, and if I missed anything at all that was it. After a while I was afraid to splurge on a tube of toothpaste, and every day when I counted up my money it was less than I thought it would be.

Down at the button store, where they had all the psychedelic and astrology stuff, a bunch of notes were pinned up on the wall. There were requests for rides to California, personal messages, and also listings of places to live. Some of the notices were way out and really made me laugh, like the one from a guy who wanted a girl to walk through the South with him dressed in Confederate clothes and carrying a musket and living off whatever they could shoot or pick in the woods. I wish Cynthia had been with me to see that one, because she'd have gotten a great kick out of it. I did miss Cynthia. The hardest thing in the world was not to phone her, but I was afraid that once I called her my parents would somehow find out and track me down. She was the one person I could laugh with. If I had thought she would come down and join me, I'd have called her in a minute, but not Cynthia. She has a pretty good setup at home, her parents leave her alone, and she's hard and practical, out to get what she can. She wouldn't have stood the cockroaches for a night, and I can see why, because no one bothers her with a lot of questions, and she and her boyfriend are beautiful together.

I looked over each of the notices, and there was one that sounded interesting. Two artists wanted a girl to come in and take care of their loft, clean up, cook one meal a day, and take care of their cats. I called them up right away, and the guy that answered said to come over. Four enormously long blocks, almost to the East River, walking against the wind through slushy streets, because it had snowed the night before, then up five flights of stairs. The halls were full of terrible smells—food, stale oil, urine—and there was garbage piled outside the doors that smelled and looked as if it had been there for days. When I got to the top floor I saw a door with a card that said D. Shawn and Henry Bolten on it. It was a wide, tin door with a number of locks. Then I got scared. Who were D. Shawn and Henry Bolten? They could be sex maniacs or white slavers. . . . I stood there with every horrible idea imaginable coming to my mind, but I didn't turn around and go back downstairs.

This was the supreme test. If I ran away now I'd be lost. It was like the night I shivered through that thunderstorm alone in the house. Even though I was a kid I knew then that if I survived I'd be stronger than Edward, stronger than I'd ever expected to be, and I could look down on Edward because he would be the weak one. I thought of Edward, as I stood in front of that door, Edward with his flashy sports car, his Brooks Brothers shirts, his tape recorder, and his eight-hundred-dollar camera. I used to be jealous of all the things he got, the way my mother fussed about him, and the look on her face when he walked into a room—a bright, shining proud look that she never had for me. The more she gave him the more I didn't want anything from her, because I knew that she was only doing her duty with me. My mother loved to say, "I treat both my children exactly alike," and she used to count out the candies and divide up the cookies, "share and share alike," but Edward always got the half of the chocolate bar that had the nuts in it. He was older and bigger and a boy, so naturally I had to understand that he needed more than I did. Like always, she mouthed phrases that said one thing while she lived, acted, and loved entirely differently. I wasn't fooled for long, and the more Edward accepted the more I wanted no part of the handouts she offered me.

It was too late now for anyone, or anything, even my own fears, to buy me off. I knocked on the door.

A short, stocky man opened it very quickly as if he must have heard me coming up the stairs and had been standing on the other side waiting. He greeted me embarrassed like, looking ill at ease, and the first thing he said was that he was sorry Mr. Bolten wasn't in. So at least I knew that he was Mr. Shawn.

I was surprised that he wasn't a kid and relieved that the place really looked like an artist's studio. It was a big, barnlike room, with enormous vivid paintings and pieces of clay sculpture strewn around. His pants were covered with about every color of paint, and his arms sticking out of his rolled-up sleeves were muscular and hairy. From the neck down he looked like a prize fighter, but his face in spite of his droopy mustache came on gentle, almost feminine. He didn't make me feel up tight at all, which was a great relief.

"You look so young," he said. "Are you sure you want to do this?"

"What would I have to do?" I could see by the dirt and the little piles of rubbish in the corner that the place hadn't been cleaned for months. But that didn't bother me, because he was like a friend, and that made me want to fix things up for him.

"We share this place, Bolten and I. I work in the daylight, because I'm a painter, and he works at night, because he's a sculptor and doesn't care about the light. There's another room, and we thought that if a girl wanted to live here, with free rent, she could kind of keep the place cleaned up, take care of the cats, and cook us a meal sometimes. We like to have dinner here together. It isn't much of a job," he said apologetically, "but you could still have a job someplace else. I mean it wouldn't take all your time."

I hadn't seen the cats, but now, as if they'd heard them-selves mentioned, two big gray cats came out from be-hind an easel and ran over to him. One jumped to his shoulder, and the other he took into his lap. "There are three kittens too. We like cats." Then I noticed that a lot of the clay figures were of the cats in different sizes and poses. At least, they don't paint nude women, I thought, and turned myself right off, because it was the kind of thing my mother would have said.

"It sounds all right to me. Could I see the room?" I felt pleased that I remembered to be businesslike enough to ask.

He took me into a tiny hallway. Off it there was a small bathroom—equipped with toilet, sink, and makeshift shower—and also a minute room just big enough for the narrow cot and dresser.

"Where do you two sleep?" I hadn't seen any beds in the other room.

"We don't live here. We just come here to work. You wouldn't be afraid to stay here alone, would you?"

"It looks like you've got enough locks on the door."

"People have tried to break in once or twice, but that was before we got all the locks. I think you'll be safe here. But I wouldn't come home alone too late at night."

I could feel myself getting scared all over again. It was going to be creepy in that barren place alone at night. "Have you got a radio?"

"Yes, we have. In the other room."

That settled it. If I could play music I'd be all right. And this was really it, really what I'd come down for, to earn my own way, to be alone, and to do some figuring. I wouldn't get any salary, but at least I'd eat and have a place to sleep by myself.

"Okay. When do you want me to start?"

"You can come today if you want."

"That's fine." We shook hands on the deal. His hand was so strong he almost crushed mine.

When I went back downstairs through that dirty, smelly hall, I got scared for real all over again. What did I know about those guys? The wind was blowing in from the East River and it tasted good. Some kids on the street were playing a game with a stick and a ball, laughing and yelling, and I passed a store filled with white bridal gowns. I made up my mind I was going to go through with it. I wasn't going to turn back like the girl who wanted a birthday cake. She was a lost one. The whole thing was chance, and I'd take mine. What did I have to lose?

I thought about Steve and wished I'd meet him walking up the street toward me. He would understand about despair.

EIGHT

"These streets are still pretty. They haven't changed."
The car was going east on Tenth Street to Fifth Avenue.
Mrs. Nichols watched a group of young girls and boys
come out of an attractive brownstone. Why couldn't my
Claudia be like that? Her eyes followed the group envi-
ously as they walked down the block, talking and laughing. "When Claudia comes home, perhaps we should take

a little apartment down here. She could come in for weekends."

"*If* Claudia comes home." Mr. Nichols slammed on the brakes as a taxi pulled out from the curb in front of him. "Damn those taxi drivers!"

"Don't frighten me, David. Of course, she'll come home."

"Don't be so sure."

"Watch where you're going." He slammed on the brakes again as the light turned red. "You're making me very nervous. What makes you think she won't come home?"

"I don't know what I think. We have to find her first. Damn these lights."

"You were the one who talked about being calm. I was counting on you to be calm. David, I keep thinking about such terrible things—all the muggings and rapes in the newspaper—but it doesn't look so bad. I'm just talking, David, because I'm scared. You'll have to let me talk. See, Washington Square doesn't look so awful. There are women with baby carriages, and I don't mind the long hair, some of it anyway. All our male models wear their hair long, and they're perfectly nice boys."

"Fags."

"That's not true. One of them, no older than Edward, asked me to have lunch with him. A darling boy and with such exquisite taste. He knew immediately what was wrong with the props we'd set up. It's dead, he said, no drama, no excitement. You need lots of flowers and color. You know, I have a wild idea. Do you suppose Roger Ferris is queer? Claudia acted so oddly about him the night before she left." Mrs. Nichols pinched her husband's arm. "My God, maybe I've hit on something. Maybe that's why she left. It would be awful for a girl to discover she was in love with a fag."

"I don't think Claudia gave a damn about Roger Ferris. He never looked you straight in the eye when he shook hands."

"That's what I mean. Poor boy. . . ."

"Jean, you're talking yourself into something. You're letting your imagination run wild."

"What's wrong with imagination? That's why I'm a good editor." Mrs. Nichols paused and peered apprehensively at the tenements as they rode south on MacDougal Street.

"We'll be damned lucky if we find her at that girl Myrna's," Mr. Nichols said, pulling the car abruptly into an empty parking space.

Arty shops in basements and first floors of broken-down houses. Boutique dresses amid Victorian lampshades, leather sling chairs, boots, belts, and bags. . . .

"Oh, God, I'm in a state. I can't believe this is us, down here on a Sunday afternoon looking for our daughter. At least, Mother's not with us. I couldn't have stood it if she'd come along. She kept looking at me as if I'd committed a crime. David, do you think Claudia will be here?"

"We'll soon find out." He pressed the bell marked Lowe, and they both listened to it echo in the dark hallway.

"I have no idea where she is." Myrna was dressed in dirty slacks and a boy's shirt. Hugh was eating an apple and spitting seeds into a cluttered ashtray. He did not offer Mrs. Nichols his chair.

"But she *was* here?" Mrs. Nichols repeated the question for the third time, her eyes searching the room as if she might discover Claudia behind a piece of furniture.

"I've told you everything I know. I'm not keeping anything from you. I wouldn't want that responsibility. Yes, she did come here, but then she left." Her eyes turned to Hugh. "It was too crowded."

Mrs. Nichols's eyes opened wide. "Did she, did she stay here with the two of you?"

Myrna laughed. "You *are* funny, Mrs. Nichols."

"Do you mean you can't help us?" Mr. Nichols's hand on his wife's arm tightened.

"I'm afraid not. I'm sorry. And I think Claudia really wants to be left alone. A lot of the kids don't, but she's different."

"Was she all right?" Mrs. Nichols wriggled in her husband's grasp.

"She seemed to be fine. Moody, you know the way Claudia is."

"Well, she's probably in the East Village someplace." Mr. Nichols relighted his cigar with a nervous hand.

Myrna picked up one of the cats and cradled it in her arms. "You'd better try the button stores, the book shop, the food kitchen, and the Spot, a lot of the kids hang out there. I suppose you've contacted the Fifth Precinct. They know what's going on."

"What would she be living on? She had very little money. . . ."

"She had some money with her. Maybe she got a job." Myrna looked up and met Mr. Nichols's eyes. "It's a bad scene down here, Mr. Nichols, and some kids get into awful trouble. I can't tell you that Claudia's okay, because I don't know. She could have stayed here if she wanted to, but she left."

"Why didn't you call us when she came? You might have done that."

"Come on, Mrs. Nichols. It wasn't my business to call you. All you parents are the same. You want to blame everything and everyone, but yourselves. I'm not saying it was your fault that Claudia ran away, but don't try to put it on me."

"Claudia looked up to you."

"Bully for her. I'm doing all right. I've got a job. I'm not taking anything from anyone." She let the cat go, and he leaped up on the bookcase.

Mr. and Mrs. Nichols left and climbed back into the Mercedes. "I wonder if her parents know she's living with that boy."

"Oh, for God's sake! Who cares?"

"Sorry." They both stared ahead of them silently.

A journey into nowhere. A big, black shiny Mercedes, a lady in a mink coat, and a man in a Karakul fur hat. Dark-skinned children crawling over the car. "They have such sad beautiful eyes, David." "They're scratching up the car." Insolent-faced beatniks, hippies, yippies with suspicious eyes. "No, we haven't seen anyone looks like her."

In and out of dark, incense-smelling shops, high heels tapping on cold pavements, hope and fear on a lopsided seesaw, candlelighted coffee shops, the clinging, musty odor of marijuana, the wind across Tompkins Square, a jagged piece of wood stuck·on top of a pile of dirt naming it Hoving Hill, shabby tenements and beer saloons, a quick brandy from a fat, grim-faced bartender, a flashing neon sign announcing *Electric Circus*, another small handwritten sign saying *Wednesday Night, Hard Rock Music Only a Dollar*, a bare corner store with poster-decorated windows begging one and all to come to art classes, writing classes, music classes, Spanish and English classes, *Self-Development Makes a Happy Community*, red-faced winos and serious-eyed youngsters begging for a quarter, a dime. "A husky young fellow like you should go out and get a job." "What did you give him, David?" Cards and beads and signs of the zodiac spread out on a counter, posters of old movie stars and revolutionary heroes. *Your Material or Ours. Your Design or Ours. Delicatessen and Dairy. Queen of Hearts, Will Open at 9 P.M. British East. The Wood Bowl. . . .*

"I'm exhausted."
"I know. We'll just stop at the police station, and then go to the hotel."

"It's such a jungle, David. I'm so scared."

"Edward should have come with me. It's too much for you. I don't think he really cares."

"That's not true. Edward adores Claudia. And she him. That's what worries me so. I'm sure if she were all right she would have called him. She loves Edward."

"I wonder. If she really wanted to get away she wouldn't call anyone."

"But those two have a good relationship. It's something that I cherish. Most kids fight so. Helen Matthews and I talk about it all the time. She can't believe that our two get along so well together, and she says that Claudia is bound to call Edward."

"Did you tell her?"

"Well, not exactly. I told her that Claudia took off to stay with a friend, and that we hadn't heard from her. I had to tell her something. You can't imagine what it's been like at the office, trying to keep things going and being worried sick all the time. I had to talk to someone."

"There's nothing wrong with telling anyone, and I don't know why you lie about what's happened."

"It wasn't exactly a lie. Maybe she *is* with a friend. She was with that Myrna girl. Oh, I can't bear to think of our little girl down here. She still is my baby after all. . . ."

"If any of these hippie boys lays a hand on her, I'll kill

him. I swear I will." Mr. Nichols pulled the Mercedes to a stop in front of the police station. The tires rubbed against the curb and gently he eased the car a safe six inches away.

"Yeah, we got a file on Claudia Nichols. Nothing's turned up on her yet. We have hundreds of these cases and we do what we can. It's a jungle down here, and if these kids want to get lost they manage to. But sooner or later she'll turn up. They almost always do."

"She's been gone over a week already. We're worried sick. There must be something you can do." He doesn't really care. She's not his daughter. No one really cares. Jean Nichols twisted her black-kid gloves in her hands and tried a smile on the tired-faced police officer. "I know you people are terribly efficient, we think you do a wonderful job, but she's so young, our only daughter. You must understand. . . ."

"I understand. You're the fifth pair of parents been here today. The kids usually take off on a weekend. We'll keep trying. You too. Just go around, and you'll spot her. They all come out on the streets."

"It seems impossible, this day and age, that a girl can completely disappear."

"It's part of this day and age."

From their room in an old-fashioned, shabby hotel on East Eleventh Street, Mrs. Nichols looked out over the roof tops across the street. "Let's get out of here. It's so depressing, and I need a drink. I think we ought to call Edward tonight and insist that he come down tomorrow. I'd feel better if he were here."

"I really don't see any point in disrupting his life too. He has his papers to do, and then exams. There's nothing he can do that we can't."

"I thought you were the one who thought he should be here."

"I thought he ought to *want* to come. That's different."

"Well, I need him." After all her care never to fight with David, they seemed to be at each other constantly this past, horrible week. She always had thought that a crisis brought people together. Once she had run a good piece in the magazine on the subject. With a shudder she remembered her associate editor's caustic reaction: "Depends on what two people have to start with. Nothing plus nothing still adds up to nothing."

NINE

Saturday night I almost decided to go home. Everything seemed useless, and it didn't matter where I lived. I lay awake most of the night trying to fathom out the reason for my existence. I didn't feel I had to have some *important purpose* to my life—I'm not that conceited and I don't believe I was put on earth for any special reason—but there seemed to be no meaning to life itself. There must be more to it than buying things (my mother), than working and paying bills (my father), than thinking of only yourself and having a good time (my brother), than being absolutely alone and useless (me).

Nothing down on the East Side was the way I expected it to be. I thought of all the phony love stuff on Valentine's Day when I took off, and, believe me, it's just as phony here. At least, it is for me. Perhaps if you ever find love, it gives a meaning to life. If a guy like Steve, which of course is a wild fantasy, ever really loved me, I know I would feel entirely different about everything. When I was utterly depressed I kept thinking that if he honestly wanted to find me he could, and then other times I told myself that that was impossible. Even Myrna didn't know where I was, not that she cared.

But there I was more or less living with those two queers. It was the strangest arrangement and made me feel more alone than ever. They truly tried to be nice to me, telling me not to lug heavy groceries up all those flights of stairs and asking me if I had enough heat. I would have died, though, without the radio. It was the only comfort I had lying in my own room with the door locked listening to the music.

But I didn't have anyplace else to go anyway, so I stayed on and cleaned the studio up and cooked them their one meal a day, and the cats were great. Sometimes

Bolten and Shawn were a lot of fun, making their beautifully right comments on the scene. They were both terribly bright and quick with a comeback.

It made me laugh to think that I was working for queers. My mother would have had a fit. With all her sophistication and thinking she was with it, she always got a funny look on her face when anyone said the word *homosexual*, as if it were a dirty word that no one should say out loud. I think she would have preferred my sleeping with Roger Ferris to living with those two.

The thing was I felt safe with them, which was the best part. I couldn't walk down the street or into any of the hangouts without someone trying to pick me up, and I wasn't going to have any of that. I never had thought I was afraid of sex, but when it was there, all around me, I was scared stiff. Maybe I'm a misfit, although this girl Louise, who worked at the Service Organization—the SO —said she felt the same way. She absolutely had to have love first before she wanted anyone to come near her. It wasn't being afraid only, but disgusted by the idea of making love with anyone who wasn't fantastically right. And the creeps who made repulsive remarks on the streets were horrible, drunks and dope addicts and awful people. They wore crazy costumes, with things wound around their heads, long capes, torn pants, and different colored shoes. Some even went barefoot in the snow. At times I thought I was walking through an insane asylum. It was a terrible scene, and perhaps I would have left if I hadn't kept hoping I'd find Steve again. I kept looking for him everywhere.

Sometimes I went into the church at Saint Marks Place. It was warm and quiet, and it seemed that I could think better there. I thought about all the kids down in the Village. Surely they had come for some reason. Yet everyone was so busy doing his own thing and being up tight about something that no one was making things better for others. I thought about God when I sat in the church, but I decided He couldn't exist. After all, the world was a mess. Still, if a swinging Jesus Christ came along and united all the kids, then the world could truly be a beautiful place. The thought got me excited, and I was dying to discuss it with someone, but there was no one to talk to.

Even Louise said she was so lonesome she put up a sign on the bookstore with her telephone number, and asked anyone to call anytime. Yet when a boy did call, she was afraid to give out her address and to ask him to come over, because he could be a sex maniac. No one wanted to get raped and thrown down an elevator shaft, the way one girl was found.

East Village was a scary place to live, but I learned
that if you kept away from the junkies and the kids who
were on LSD and other things, and if you managed without begging on the streets, your chances were better. I
had no desire to go to California, because I still was hoping against hope I'd find Steve. Going home would be
deathville, something worse than going back into prison,
so I stayed on.

But then, Bolten and Shawn started arguing with each
other. After a few really funny wisecracks, one of them
would say something mean that got the other one mad.
Soon they'd be screaming at each other so nastily I'd go
into my room and be scared to come out. One night Mr.
Bolten slammed out of the place, and Mr. Shawn went to
work breaking up most of Mr. Bolten's cat figures. I tried
to get him to stop, but of course he told me to mind my
own business. I couldn't stand staying there watching
him, and I was terribly afraid of what would happen
when Mr. Bolten came back, so I went out.

I picked up Louise at the SO, and since it was a
Wednesday night, we decided to blow ourselves to an
evening at the Spot, where we could listen to some music
for a dollar apiece plus money for a coke. The Spot was a
hippie hangout, but it was okay. The funny thing was
that there in the soft light, listening to the music and

sometimes the poetry read aloud, the world became beautiful. You forgot the fights and the nastiness, and believed for a little while that there were some people who really cared about beauty and love. You could get high just drinking a coke, because the music tore you up until this thing that was happening got so big you knew that no one could stop it. I wanted to write poetry, I wanted to be a beautiful person, I wanted to love. And I wanted to cry, because I guess I'd thought when I got on that train at Stony Point that I'd find someone, someone like Steve, who would see behind my skinniness and my stupid hair and my shyness and find me beautiful. I mean the real me.

"I'm going home." Louise struck me dumb.

"But why?"

"Listen, I came here for the kicks, for an experience, but after what happened to that girl I'm scared. It's a bad scene, and I'm homesick. You won't believe it, but I miss my sister and my kid brother. We used to have some fun at home."

I was wildly jealous of Louise. Her father, who worked the family farm; her mother, who worked in a factory; her sister and her brother. And the letters she got from her boyfriend. She had something to go home to. Again I was set apart. I hadn't come for the kicks. I'd come because I had to get out of the suffocating air of Stony Point. I'd come to find another way of living, to find someone to love and to love me, to find some kind of a meaning in my life. But I wasn't getting very far, and when the music became sad the loneliness wrapped itself around me so that even plump, solid, friendly Louise became a stranger. All the beautiful people were shadows in a separate world that I was looking at from the outside like a kid with his nose pressed against a pastry-shop window.

"I'll walk you as far as Avenue D," Louise said.

When I left her at the corner the block ahead looked dark, as if it stretched on forever like those frightening corridors you run through in nightmares. Louise said, "Walk near the curb away from the hallways. And don't run."

About a third of the way down the block I saw three boys come out of a building across the street, and they called out to me. I paid no attention and went on walking, praying that there'd be someone else around, but there wasn't a soul. I walked fast, and they kept up with me on the other side, laughing and calling out obscenities. I thought of the dark hallway I was going to enter, and the five flights of stairs, and I knew if they wanted to overtake me I wouldn't stand a chance. If I turned around and went back, though, I might make it safely to the Spot.

I was terrified, but I kept pretending not to notice the boys. They looked pretty young, as far as I could tell, so I kept telling myself they were just kids and wouldn't really do anything to me. But they were big, and when I started to walk faster, they laughed louder and asked me where I was running to. Then I heard one of them say, "Come on. What are we waiting for? Let's cross the street."

That was one time in my life that I wished a cop had appeared. I didn't care about anything except getting away from those boys. I was almost back to Avenue D where at least there were some lights, and I was running like mad, but I was no match for them. They caught up with me and crazily I ducked into a hallway where I heard music playing.

I tried to scream, but one of them put his hand over my mouth. I kicked and fought, and all the while they were saying horrible things that I'll never forget as long as I live. They pulled off my coat and were tugging at my sweater, when glory be to God a woman called out from the apartment. "Stop that noise. I'm calling the police, 911. They'll be here in seconds."

The boys dropped me like a hot potato, but one of

them kicked me before they ran and picked up my pocketbook. It had all the money I owned in it. I sat on the floor crying. Then I kind of crawled over to the apartment of the woman who had called out and pounded on the door, asking her to let me in.

"I'm not opening the door for anyone. Get out of here. We don't want no tramps around here."

"Are the cops coming?"

She laughed. "Oh yeah, they're coming." And I knew she hadn't called them at all. The people in that neighborhood didn't call the cops often.

I sat there crying for I don't know how long. While I'd been running I'd been scared, but kind of all right. Then, when I could think and realized what a close call I'd had, I fell into a panic. It was unbelievable to realize that three strange boys who'd never laid eyes on me before had decided on the spur of the moment to hurt me. Rape was in their eyes, and even murder. I wrapped my coat around me, but I couldn't stop shivering. Oh, God, I thought, maybe if I were dead I'd be better off. But I didn't want to die yet, and not that way. . . .

I could hear noises from the apartment. The radio was still playing, and that woman's harsh voice was speaking to someone else. She'd saved my life, but I never would know what she looked like. I could pass her on the street a hundred times and I wouldn't know her. That made me feel worse again, as if I didn't really exist except to be knocked down in a hallway and trampled on. Someone had said "Don't," but didn't care any more than that. Like don't step on that caterpillar.

Then when I thought about my money and the things I'd lost in my pocketbook, I started to cry all over again. I couldn't imagine what I'd do without any money, and the loss itself seemed to have taken away the last hold I had on my identity. I mean I had nothing. I had to tell myself that I still had a name, Claudia Nichols.

After a while I managed to stand up and peek out the door. Those boys weren't in sight, but they could be hiding anywhere, and I still was scared. Sitting in that hallway was creepy, though, so I ventured outside. I certainly wasn't about to walk down that long, dark street again, and I had no desire to stay in the apartment alone or face Bolten and Shawn, so the only place that I could think of to go was Myrna's.

I don't know how I made it across town. I walked on Eighth Street, which had people and lights, huddled inside my coat, hurting all over and wondering what was to become of me. I wanted terribly to be sick, but not in the street, and I kept my mouth closed tight. At last I got to MacDougal Street and fled to Myrna's.

"Christ, you look green." It was Steve, sitting in Myrna's big chair with the cats in his lap. I wanted to fall down at his feet, not caring how terrible I looked, just so happy to see him I wanted to cry all over again.

"What happened to you?" Myrna, Hugh, and Danny were all staring at me.

"I got mugged. Over near Avenue D, in a hallway. They took my pocketbook, but I'm all right. I really am." After I caught my breath I told them everything.

"You're a stupid fool to be out alone in these streets at night. How dumb can you be?" Steve was furious.

Myrna gave me a shot of whiskey. I hated the taste, but I drank it down and it felt good and warm inside me. Then she took me into the bedroom. "Those boys didn't do anything to you, did they?"

"They didn't have a chance. But they ripped my coat and sweater, and took my money. It's all gone, I haven't a penny now." In Myrna's mirror I could see the mess I was.

"You're lucky." Myrna was scowling. "Your parents were here. They're out looking for you."

"You didn't tell them anything, did you?"

"I didn't have anything to tell them. I don't know where you've been. And I don't want to know either. I think you'd better call them."

"I can't. Not yet. They'll make me go home."

"What are you going to do?"

"I don't know. I'll find something." I didn't tell Myrna about Bolten and Shawn, because I didn't want to go back there. And I wasn't going to call my parents until I had something, something to show them that I could take care of myself and be on my own. Now I had nothing. When I rode down on that train I'd had all kinds of ideas: living in a nice commune, being part of a group, working together with other kids. I had no idea the Village was going to be like this, that there was no nice commune, that I was going to be so alone in a crazy jungle.

Back in the other room, she said, "Danny's sleeping on the couch. He's got a bum back. But you can have the floor if you want to stay."

"She can come back with me," Steve said.

Any other time those words would have torn me up, but the way he said them made me feel like I was something to be put up with. Taken care of like a kid left on a doorstep.

Myrna gave Steve a hard look. "She's a kid, Steve. Only sixteen."

He laughed. "Yeah, I know." He didn't say I'd told him I was eighteen, and I was grateful for that. I would have been grateful for anything that night even the Salvation Army.

I had a hard time keeping up with Steve's long steps. He didn't say a word to me all the way home, but he kept a tight hold on my arm.

TEN

Jean Nichols sat at her desk and absentmindedly watched her secretary arrange a small bouquet of lilies of the valley in a blue vase. She was staring at the flowers hard, making Miss Janis wonder uncomfortably if she were doing something wrong, but Mrs. Nichols's mind was occupied elsewhere. The two-day search through the village had proved fruitless. Nothing had been accomplished except two parking tickets for the Mercedes, the wearing out of a pair of expensive Italian shoes, a huge pileup of work on her desk, and a severe migraine headache.

Restlessly Mrs. Nichols pushed away from the desk and stood up. "The flowers look lovely," she murmured, transferring her gaze from the vase to Miss Janis. Why hadn't she a daughter like her? A soft, feminine figure, a scrubbed, radiant face, and an eye for fashion and her future that was going to take her far from her Kansas City home and a dinky junior college. A single-minded ambition to get ahead that Jean Nichols was watching develop with profound admiration. Estelle Janis was a representative of the younger generation about whom Mrs. Nichols loved to write, and she could spin endless smooth, graceful sentences about how this charming, educated, new generation all-American girl found time to visit museums, read the latest books, go to the films and the theater, hold down an eight-hour-a-day responsible job, join a political party, attract a devoted boyfriend, take her grandmother to the park, and dress fashionably on a limited salary without showing any strain. At appropriate seasons of the year Mrs. Nichols's crystal ball would predict the long and happy lives of the Estelle Janises of America, the charming engagement parties they would be given, the girlish showers, the small but elegant weddings, the ranch-style houses they would live in, the furnishings, down to the intimacies of the bathroom, they would buy, the families they would plan carefully, and the various kinds of baby food they would have on their kitchen shelves.

Estelle Janis represented a clean, wholesome, and ordered world, the world sought after by Jean Nichols, and for the hundredth, or thousandth time, she asked herself how she had mothered a child who preferred an unclean, sick, disgusting underworld instead.

She walked out of her office and into that of her associate editor, Helen Matthews. She knew when she perched on the edge of Helen's desk that she was going to talk more than she should. But she didn't care. It was impossible to keep everything bottled up any longer, and she desperately needed a woman to confide in. She and David were repeating the same platitudes at home, each aware of his own increasing nervousness and tension, and leaving the crucial things unsaid.

"What's the matter? You've been in a funk all week. Marital troubles?" Helen Matthews's long, slim fingers picked up a cigarette, and then put it down, unlighted. "No, I'm going to resist. I'm allowing myself two cigarettes at cocktail time, and that's all." She was a pale-faced woman, younger than Jean, whose long, sensitive face was made severe by the modish, short cut of her crisp black hair. The effect was not pretty but striking.

"If that were only all. Something much worse. I told you Claudia was visiting a friend. She's not. She's left home, she's a runaway." Mrs. Nichols stared bleakly at her friend, her eyes filling with tears. "I can't say the word without crying. I hate it. When I was young, *runaway* used to mean a horse to me. A runaway horse. Now it's kids. . . ."

Helen rose and put her arms around Mrs. Nichols. "I'm so sorry, so terribly sorry. I don't know what to say. I'm kind of stunned. Cry if you want to. You've been holding it in, and you probably need a good cry."

"I've been crying all week," Mrs. Nichols sobbed. "I can't seem to stop. Poor David is disgusted with me, but it's been so ghastly. You can't imagine. . . ."

"Oh, I can. I know what you must be going through. You're terrific to have come to work. I don't know what I'd do if anything happened to my kids."

"Coming to work is easier than staying home." Mrs. Nichols blew her nose into a tissue and dried her face. "The awful thing is we don't know what to do next." She described what they had done so far. "It seems like so little, and the helplessness is so awful." She moved over to the window and glanced out. "I walk along the streets thinking I'll see her. I'm always looking."

"She's such a beautiful girl. I still can't believe it."

Mrs. Nichols turned around from the window. "Do you think she's beautiful? I wouldn't have said so. I always thought she was interesting looking, but beautiful . . . no. I'd do anything, though, to see her face now."

"She *is* beautiful. And when she gets a little older she'll be more so. She has such an exciting face, so mobile. Her expression is always changing when she talks to you."

"Not with me it doesn't. I draw a blank." Mrs. Nichols moved around the room restlessly, picking up a book and putting it down, changing around the finely carved statuettes on Mrs. Matthews's bookshelf. Abruptly her eyes met Mrs. Matthews's. "Claudia doesn't like me. I've never admitted this to anyone, not even myself."

"Do you like Claudia?" Mrs. Matthews pulled her eyes away and looked down at her desk.

"I love her. Of course, I love her. I want her to have everything, to be a happy girl."

"But liking is different. You can love a child and still not really like her."

"That's ridiculous, Helen. Claudia's my only daughter, and you know I'd do anything in the world for her."

"You still haven't answered my question, but forget it. I do know what you're going through, but she'll come back. You'll hear from her."

"That's what everyone says. But *when?* I wake up in the middle of the night in a cold sweat thinking about all the things that could be happening to her. I try to busy myself working, but my thoughts wander."

"Why don't you take some time off?"

Mrs. Nichols shook her head. "No. I'd go out of my mind if I weren't working."

"Speaking of work, I was going to speak to you this morning—about that interview on the Betsy Dillon program. The taping is set for tomorrow morning." Mrs. Matthews consulted some papers on her desk. "You're supposed to be at the studio at ten o'clock."

"Oh my God, I forgot about it." She stopped in front of the antique gold mirror behind Mrs. Matthews's desk and examined her tearstained face. "I don't know if I can do it."

"I can pinch-hit for you, but you're much better on TV than I am. And I think it would do you good."

Mrs. Nichols continued to stare at her face. "I look

ghastly. I'll have to get my hair done today. . . . I suppose the show must go on. Do you really and truly believe we'll hear from her soon?" Her voice was pleading, like a child's.

"Yes, I think you will."

Mrs. Nichols sat under the drier trying to make notes for her television interview. One question was sure to be what she thought of the younger generation. What did she think of the campus rebellions?

What could she say? She felt a sudden panic, alarmed that the question itself might set her off into tears and that her mind would go blank with only Claudia's pale face and masked eyes taunting her. The sureness of her editorial hand became strangely shaken, and she found herself groping for the right words and phrases that usually slipped off her pen so easily. What *was* behind all of today's rebellion? These kids hadn't seen the breadlines or felt the hunger and the poverty that she had. To gain financial security had been for her the most important thing. To make a good marriage and also to find an interesting job, to be able to buy pretty things and pay the bills had seemed a lot to her when she was Claudia's age.

She could see the ghetto kids and the blacks complaining, they had something to complain about, but what did the kids who had the good homes, the pretty clothes and cars and record players have to shout about? She felt a wave of indignation against their jibes and mockery, against their condemnation of the very system that was providing them with so much. Her generation had pulled themselves up out of a depression and survived a world war, and they were supplying the money for the colleges and universities, for the trips to Europe, for the books and the psychoanalyses and all the good things in life these kids needed to be healthy and happy. Yet what *they* wanted to do was to tear down.

She was faltering no longer and started writing furiously on her yellow pad. As editor, she had defended the younger generation in the magazine, had tried to make excuses and gone along with those who said that every younger generation had to rebel and that the materialistic values in America were lacking in spiritual and humanistic goals. But now she was angry, and the anger felt good. She became excited by her own emotion and lashed out with her pen against those youngsters who were trying to destroy the world she and her peers had fashioned. Of course, it wasn't a perfect world, but what generation hadn't been faced with wars and strife and problems? It felt good to have the sentences come swiftly and easily, to find so readily the positive accomplishments society had to offer. Jean Nichols barely looked up from her pad, and for the first time since Claudia had left home her attention was fully and confidently involved in the job before her.

On the train home that evening, Mrs. Nichols with excitement in her voice read to her husband some of the notes she had made for her interview the following morning. "What do you think?"

"You've certainly made a switch. Aren't you being a bit subjective?"

He never said the right thing to her. "There's nothing wrong with changing one's ideas. You can call it subjective, but I say I've learned a lesson. When our daughter leaves a home like ours, she's done something destructive to you and me and to herself, to a family unit. And I don't think it should be condoned. We have worked too hard to be put through so much agony. And why?"

"You're making judgments that are premature. But I suppose what you've got is good material for an interview, even if I don't agree."

He had a talent for deflating her, for picking holes in her enthusiasms and ideas. But she was not to be talked out of her beliefs this time. If she could hold on to her anger perhaps she would not break into tears every time she thought of all the horrors that could be happening to her girl.

Mrs. Nichols read the notes over to herself, and that night she closeted herself in her bedroom, asking not to be disturbed, and practiced saying her words aloud.

When she was finished she could not resist the pull, which she felt every evening, to go into Claudia's room. Later Mr. Nichols found her sitting there in the dark. He touched her shoulder gently with his hand.

"I'm glad you can keep busy working."

"I'd die if I couldn't." She turned her face up to him. "David, isn't there something more that we can do?"

"Edward said he'd go down to the Village this weekend, didn't he?"

She nodded. "What about the people you know? The judges. . . . Can't someone put some pressure on the Police Commissioner? How do we know the police are really working on the case?"

"I'll call a few people, although I'm sure the police are doing what they can."

"Promise me you'll call."

"I promise."

He was already out of the room when she called out "David," softly. She knew her voice was too low for him to hear, but with a sigh that was close to a sob she didn't try again. In a little while, from memory, she spoke her words aloud once more. She hoped that they would not keep repeating themselves in her head all night long.

ELEVEN

When Steve opened the door to his apartment, reached around me to switch on the light, and then waited for me to come in, I had the weirdest sensation of having done all this before. It was a crazy feeling, because you know I'd never been anywhere near his place, but maybe I had gone into a safe haven with someone like Steve before in my dreams.

"You want some hot soup?"

"Yeah, that would be great."

The room was like Steve, big and comfortable and not jazzed up. No posters on the walls, no junk around, and it was terribly clean. It wasn't like most boys' rooms—my brother Edward left his in a worse mess than I did—but it was very male just the same, almost monklike with white walls and a big, flat door on some cement blocks for a desk, a couple of dark sofa beds, an oak table, and a few chairs. There was a screen in a corner and behind it an old-fashioned refrig and an electric grill. There were a lot of books, a record player, and a very small TV set. I loved that room.

While we sat there drinking some kind of thick soup out of his big mugs, I stopped shivering for a bit. I guess I was in a state of shock after what had happened to me, because I couldn't think about anything else besides the warmth and safety of the room. It was really weird after all the fantasies I'd had about Steve that there I was in his apartment alone with him in the middle of the night and the most important thing I could feel was the hot soup going down into my belly. It was like eating ice cream after you've had your tonsils out, wonderful to know that you could swallow again without its hurting.

"Come back" he said. "You're far away."

Hearing him speak to me like that, as if we were old

friends, woke me up a little. "Those boys' eyes. . . . I keep seeing them. And that woman in the apartment, I keep wondering what kind of nut she was. You know, pretending to call the police, saving my life, I guess, and then not opening the door."

"The city's full of nuts." When he smiled, his whole face crinkled up. "Kids like you shouldn't be running around loose."

"I wasn't running around."

He filled up my mug again with some more soup, and we just sat and looked at each other. I guess I was coming back to life, because it suddenly struck me that there was only one room and I got terribly nervous. Where was I going to sleep and where was he going to sleep, and had he asked me back to his place because he felt sorry for me or did he like me a little and what was going to happen? Of all the nights in the world for me to be there with him this was about the worst, because if he came near me or touched me I was sure I'd start crying. I couldn't bear anyone touching me after those horrible boys had had their hands on me, and their filthy words were still ringing in my ears.

"If you have a bathtub, I wish I could take a bath."

"Yes, sure, of course. I have a bathtub."

Then Steve got terribly efficient. He gave me a towel

and a bathrobe, and he scrubbed out the tub, although I told him I could do that, and he told me to go ahead and take a hot bath. It felt good stretched out in the hot water, and I looked at the few things he had on the bathroom shelf: his razor and shaving cream and a comb and brush. I felt terribly close to him, but shaky about what to expect or what could happen.

I put on my underwear under the bathrobe, which of course was miles too big for me, but it was his and snuggly and great, and when I went back to the other room he had cleared away the table and had put on some records. I curled up on one of the couches and listened to the music.

"I was lucky you were there tonight," I finally said. "It was nice of you to bring me back here." I sounded stupid and formal, which made me feel shy and ashamed. I thought about how awful I must look, so skinny in his big robe and my hair a mess. Without my pocketbook, I didn't have any mascara or comb or anything. Although I had used his comb in the bathroom, it didn't help much.

"Yeah. God knows why I did. I've been avoiding you."

I was truly surprised. "But you haven't seen me, so how could you avoid me?"

"I've seen you a few times, but I made sure you didn't see me."

"I'm sorry. Do you want me to go?" I started getting up. His words really hurt me.

"Don't be an idiot." He sat down on the other end of the couch. "It's just that I don't want to get involved. And I know how I react to girls like you. I'm a softie, a sucker for problems. I like to play God and fix up people's lives, but my own's too much of a mess."

"I'm not asking you to fix up my life. Or to get involved. It was nice of you to ask me here to spend the night, and I appreciate it. But don't worry. I won't hang around tomorrow. You didn't have to warn me." I was close to tears.

"You're stupid," he said softly. He came closer to me on the couch, and I moved away. "You're stupid," he repeated. "And I'm an idiot. I shouldn't have asked you up here tonight." He banged his hand against his head. "Real dumb."

I got up from the couch, holding the robe tight around me. "Thanks a lot. I don't have to stay." I started walking toward the bathroom where I'd left the rest of my clothes. The tears were smarting my eyes.

In a second he was beside me, turning me around to face him, his hands on my shoulders. I'm pretty tall, but I really had to look up to see his eyes.

"You're such a kid." He touched my wet cheek. "I knew

that first night I met you I was going to get into trouble with you. I know myself very well, all the signals. You're an innocent, and you haven't the vaguest idea of what you've got, but you've got it, and it hooks a guy like me. You can't go around with that face and that intensity and that crazy gliding walk of yours and not get into trouble."

I was trembling in his hold. I couldn't tell from his face whether he was going to kiss me or hit me. He was the one who was intense, so intense that he frightened me.

Then he kissed me. I'd never been kissed like that before in my life. It was a clean kiss, if you know what I mean, not soft and mushy like Roger Ferris, but strong and lasting, as if it would never end and he was putting the big, shaggy whole of him into it. I don't know what they mean when they say a girl melts into a boy's arms, because I didn't melt at all, I came to life right from my toes on up to the top of my head, with every part of my being I kissed him back.

Then we stood apart, and I realized he was as flustered as I was. Or maybe disturbed is a better word. And I was frightened. I was terrified of what he might expect of me, of what the next move would be. I didn't want to be a baby and make a fool of myself, and yet I knew somewhere inside of me that I didn't want to sleep with him.

Not tonight. Not with anyone, not yet. I wasn't ready and I was afraid.

"Don't look so scared," he said, and gently he led me back to the couch and sat down close beside me, still holding on to my hand. "I'm not going to rape you."

"How do you know you'd have to?" It was a halfhearted joke and stupid.

"Don't put on with me. Don't pretend to be sophisticated. I'm not going to make love to you. Not that it wouldn't be easy, believe me, but. . . ." Abruptly he stood up.

"No, it wouldn't be easy," I told him, looking up at him, "because the answer is no anyway." I almost had to laugh at the mixture of expressions that crossed his face—relief, hurt, and resentment—and I was relieved to have said it.

"You're pretty sure of yourself, aren't you? Maybe that's what I like about you—you have some guts. Well, relax. You don't have to be afraid."

"You mean we'll be friends?"

"Hell, no. We'll never just be friends. There's too much going between us." He sat down on one of the chairs, a safe distance away. "I have problems and you have problems, and for some crazy reason I don't want us to get in a mess. Maybe it's your innocence, I don't know. Maybe I'm falling in love, whatever that is. And I'm making no promises for the future, I'm no saint, but we have problems we have to work out first."

"Like what?" I'd never known any boy so sure of himself. When he spoke about having problems, you felt he was facing them and doing something about them. Never once had he asked me how I felt about him, but maybe it was written all over my face, or he knew it when we kissed. I didn't care, because that was what was so great about him. He skipped the obvious and got to the point without any pretending.

"Like where you're going to live."

"My leg's getting cramped again," I said, trying to unwind it from the way I'd been sitting on it. We both laughed remembering how we'd met, and he took hold of my leg and rubbed it like crazy.

I looked at him. "You're afraid if you . . . get involved with me I'll stay on here?" I was impressed with my own sudden hunch.

"Could be one reason."

"You act as if I have nothing to say about any of this, as if it's all up to you."

"Well, isn't it?" He looked directly into my eyes. "You're sixteen, Myrna told me. You haven't a dime to your name, you're alone in the city, and you've no place to go. I'm nineteen, and no monster—I believe you rather like me. I've got an apartment and a few bucks. I even have a part-time job. It wouldn't be too hard to persuade you to stay. Would it?"

"No, I guess not." I looked away from him. I felt unsure of him once more. Was he pretending to like me, putting on because he was afraid I'd turn out to be a burden, or was he for real? I changed my mind. "Then again I think not. I didn't leave home because I was hung up on sex. I could shack up with a guy if I wanted to. (What was I saying? I didn't believe it for a minute.) But that's not what I came for."

"What did you come for?"

I lay back on the cushions and closed my eyes, feeling the exhaustion and the tensions of the evening take over. I couldn't start telling him now. Either he knew or he didn't know.

My eyes were still closed when I felt him kiss me lightly on my lips. "Never mind. I guess you came for the same reason I did." Then I put my arms around him and he held me tight and we kissed again, for real.

Going to bed was really funny. He was like a mother hen, giving me blankets (he had no sheets), tucking me in, bathrobe and all (I didn't dare take it off), kissing me good-night, walking away and coming back to kiss me again. It was dark, and I don't think he did anything but take off his big sweater and his sneakers before he went to bed on the other couch. The whole thing was wild with him on one bed and me on the other. Who would have believed us? I thought of my mother and all her insinuations about sex, snooping around as if she wanted to confirm her worst suspicions. If you swore to her on a Bible, she'd never believe that a girl and a boy could spend the night together and not get into what she called trouble. So much for what she knew about us, or about me. She knew nothing. Most grown-ups have dirty minds, I think, always suspecting the worst.

Anyway, I was so exhausted that I fell asleep about the minute Steve turned out the lights and slept until around ten o'clock the next morning. The sun woke me up. Steve went out and bought some fresh bread, and it was beautiful sitting in his sunny window eating our breakfast together.

"Let's see if there's any news on," Steve said, turning on his tiny TV set. I nearly dropped dead, because there was my mother big as life in the picture.

"That's my mother," I told Steve. It was the weirdest sensation, as if the hand of God were putting my mother in the room there with Steve and me. It couldn't have been worse, and I guess I came as near to hating her then as I ever did with her done-up hair and face, spouting her gibberish about the younger generation. She was absolutely against us. It was the phoniest stuff I ever heard in my life, and she would have been funny if her intrusion hadn't been spoiling everything for me, which she'd always done all my life.

"Is that really your mother?" Steve laughed so hard he had to get up from the table. When the program was over, we both were laughing, although I didn't feel so good inside.

"What are you going to do?" Steve asked me.

"I don't know. What should I do?"

Then we sat and talked for hours like I'd never talked to anyone before. Steve told me he'd left college because he was wasting his time and it wasn't what he wanted to do at all. He really wanted to make movies, and when he talked about it he got excited in his understated way, you know, quiet like and serious, and he told me he had a part-time job doing lighting for some small studio that a couple of fellows operated downtown. Also, he was taking some film courses at NYU. He really was great, and the way he spoke I had a good feeling that he was going to make it and was on his way. He wasn't out to prove anything except to make his own life at what he wanted to do, and some place along the line he would settle things with his father. Settle them in a way that would get his father off his back.

"But what do *you* want to do?"

"I don't know. I wish I did. I guess I want a job."

"Then why don't you get one?"

He put me on the defensive. "I had a kind of one, except they didn't pay me anything. I don't even know where to look. I don't want the cops to pick me up."

"You're ducking the issue. Call up your folks and square that away. Then get a job."

"You're not being fair. You make it sound so easy, but it isn't. My parents will make me come home."

"Are you sure you don't want to?"

"Yes, I'm sure of that." And I was. "You saw my mother. Would you want to go home to her?"

Steve laughed. "It could be worse. But okay, you don't want to go home. Then find a job first, and then call them. If you show them you can take care of yourself, you'll have a better chance. This way you're running, but you're not going anywhere."

Steve made me feel as if I could do it. He was the first person who ever talked to me as if I weren't something to be criticized or made to feel like someone apart from other people. Even Cynthia sometimes made me feel that way. You know, okay but peculiar.

"Maybe I can help you find a job. It won't be anything glamorous or exciting, but I have a few ideas. The first thing you'd better do is call up those guys and tell them you aren't coming back. Then get dressed, and we'll go out."

He was terrific. He didn't say anything about where I was going to stay, and I didn't either. I was learning to take each day, or even each hour, as it came and not to worry about what was going to happen next.

When I came out of the bathroom dressed, he said I was a beautiful girl. Before we went out he kissed me. I wished Cynthia had been there to see us. Even Cynthia once said to me that I was the kind of girl who would be stunning when I got older, but Steve made me feel beautiful now.

First he took me over to a newspaper office. The man there said he didn't know of any jobs, and then a little later he remembered hearing that a co-op grocery store might need someone. As we walked around Steve told me a lot about the East Village that I didn't know, thinking of it only in terms of the hippies and the kids. Now a lot of the hippies were moving out, disappearing or going to houses in the country, and the people who were left were the people who had always lived there, mostly poor Puerto Ricans and blacks and Jews and Irish and Italians.

"I want to make some movies of these people, not romantic pictures of them, but real, the way it is," Steve said. "Being poor doesn't make people great, but there are some beautiful people here."

The co-op wasn't much of a store, but it was run by some people in the community who were trying to keep the prices reasonable for everyone, and so I liked the idea of working there. The man we had to see wasn't in, and they told us to come back in a couple of hours. Steve said he had to go to work, but he gave me the key to his apartment and told me to go back there. Later I could see the man, and then we could have dinner together when he came home.

It was as if we were living together when I went back to his apartment, and it was kind of marvelous going into it by myself as if I truly belonged. I put on some records and fell asleep. When I woke up, it was time to go to the store. I thought it would be nice if I could buy something for dinner, but of course I didn't have a dime.

The man at the store was very relaxed. He said yes, if I wanted to work I could have a job packing groceries, that the pay wouldn't be much, but it wasn't hard work. I asked him when he wanted me to start, and he said whenever I wanted to. He didn't ask me any questions about whether I'd ever worked before or anything. I told him I'd start the next day, so he said to come in at twelve noon, because they stayed open late that night. I was terribly excited, and I couldn't wait to tell Steve.

Steve made a great dinner of chili and salad; then he went to his class, and I stayed home. I didn't mind a bit being alone, because it was great waiting for him to come back. I wasn't nervous anymore, because I knew we'd be all right. Everything was under control, and Steve wouldn't be expecting anything of me that I wasn't ready for. I felt marvelous about the job, and in our own way things were beautiful between us. Although that night Steve said I'd better try to find a place to live, because he didn't know how long he could hold out. I understood, because he wasn't trying to get rid of me and obviously we couldn't go on living that way for long.

"When are you going to call your parents?"

I got a knot in my belly whenever I thought of them, and I'd more or less decided I'd call Edward first. But not until I had a place to live and was all set. The only trouble was I'd have to pay the first month's rent, and I didn't have any money. So Steve said he'd ask his landlord to wait a couple of weeks for his rent, which he thought he would do, and he'd lend me the money. Then when I got paid I could give it back to him. He was doing everything for me, but differently from the way my parents did. The money they gave me was never for the right thing, and there were always strings attached.

The next morning I got up very early to go out to find a place to live. The idea of living by myself was exciting. It made me feel for the first time in my life that I was in control, that I was making an important decision on my own without a lot of discussion with other people. Steve had told me what blocks to look on and what blocks to avoid because they were too rough. I trudged up and down the blocks, and up and down millions of stairs, but most of the time the superintendent wasn't around, and the apartments I did see were pretty awful.

I was ready to grab any hole in the wall when I came back to Steve's place, and then luck was with me. His janitor was out in front, and he told me he thought a girl was moving out down the block. I ran down to the building and rang the bell. Someone answered, and I ran up the four flights of stairs. The apartment wasn't anything much, two tiny rooms facing a dingy courtyard, but I could have it for fifty dollars a month, and the girl said I

could have what was in it for the total sum of another
forty. I didn't have that much money, but I said yes right
away, deciding that I'd figure something out.

I had no idea whether the bed, the blankets and sheets,
some pots and dishes, and the rickety table and chairs
were a good buy or not, but I didn't care. The furnished
apartment would be mine, and I was happy to have it.
Some paint would make it look better, and eventually I'd
fix it up on my own. I floated down the stairs and settled
the rent with the lady in the basement giving her the
money Steve had lent me.

If I'd found a million dollars on the street I couldn't
have been happier. An apartment of my own right on
Steve's block and a job all at once. It was too much.
Breathlessly I told Steve my good news.

"That's great." He was as delighted as I. "But what
about the money for the furniture? Where are you going
to get it?"

"I thought I'd call up my brother."

"You're crazy. Your brother's up in Boston, and you
told the girl you'd bring her the money this afternoon.
And what about your job? I thought you had to be there
at twelve. Calm down, baby, and think straight."

He deflated me like a balloon. "But I can't lose this. It's

too good. What should I do?" I hadn't realized how much I counted on him. "Maybe my brother could wire me the money."

"From what you've told me about your brother, I doubt he's got forty bucks lying around loose. Especially for a runaway kid sister. He's not going to send you the money to stay away."

My heart sank. "I was feeling so great. But nothing works for me. I should have known better." I sank down on the couch.

Steve came over to me and lifted up my face. "Take it easy, infant. You're too used to being beaten down, and you're also spoiled. Everything's been done for you all your life, even when you didn't like it. Listen to Papa Steve. The first thing you have to do is tell the co-op you can't start working until tomorrow. And the next thing you have to do is call up your parents. See them today and borrow the money from them."

I pulled my eyes away from his. Facing my parents was exactly what I did not want to do. I wanted desperately to take care of everything without them, not to see them until I was truly independent. To think that forty dollars stood between me and independence. I cursed those boys in my mind. If they hadn't stolen my pocketbook, I might have managed. I didn't have forty dollars in it, but I could have given that girl something and paid the rest later. If it weren't so tragic it would have been funny—to be hung up on forty bucks.

"How can I tell the co-op I can't work today when I already told him I would?" All my excitement had turned into a terrible depression. I was going to be trapped all my life. "I'll lose the job, and then I won't be able to pay for the apartment."

"I thought you had guts. But now when you have to face something real for the first time in your life, like jobs and money and a place to live, you're squelched before you start. You ran away from home, because you wanted to live your own life, to be independent, but so far you must admit you've been pretty damn well protected. You really haven't been on your own."

"But I won't be on my own if I have to borrow from my parents." I felt as if I were pleading for my life.

"Yes, you will." His voice was gentler. "Borrowing money from them doesn't mean a thing. They don't care about money. You have to be *emotionally* independent."

"You're wild. Of course, they care about money. That's all they care about. If they lend me money they'll think they own me."

"I don't give a hoot what *they* think. It's what *you* think that counts. Borrowing money doesn't let anyone own you. If you can face them with a plan of your own and stick to it, you'll be a lot freer than you are now. Borrowing the money is only incidental. Believe me, I know what I'm talking about."

I knew deep down that he was right, but I was afraid of my parents' power, afraid of myself, and afraid of giving up.

It was getting close to twelve and I had to go. "Wish me luck," I said to Steve. "I hope I don't lose the job."

"If you do you'll get another. It's not the last job in the world."

He kissed me good-bye. "I wish you luck, baby. I'm tough, but I'm rooting for you."

As I walked over to the co-op, I fingered the dime Steve had given me. One thin dime, and I'd be talking to my mother or my father. I thought I'd toss to see which one I'd call.

TWELVE

Mrs. Nichols finished the sentence in her typewriter before picking up the phone. After all the disappointments of the past three weeks she had been disciplining herself not to jump whenever the phone on her desk rang.

Her husband was at the other end, and she said hello to him in a tired voice. Then she sat up straight. "You *spoke* to Claudia! Dear God! Is she all right? Yes, of course, I'll come immediately. Luchow's? I'll jump in a taxi and come right down. David, I can't believe it."

She ran into Mrs. Matthews's office and told her the news, tears brimming her eyes. "I can't believe it," she repeated. "This is the happiest moment of my life."

She ran a comb through her hair, powdered her nose, jammed on her hat, and flung her coat around her. The taxi crawled down Park Avenue. "Don't you think it will be faster if you go down Lexington?" Obediently the driver turned into Lexington Avenue, but the traffic was just as slow. Mrs. Nichols sat back in the taxi, lighted a cigarette, and tried to quiet her thumping heart. Why had Claudia called her father? David had said Claudia was all right, but was she? What would she find? It was ridiculous to be afraid to meet her own daughter, but fear was certainly a part of her nervousness.

Jean Nichols's eyes swiftly searched the large, brightly lighted dining room. She recognized the back of Claudia's head immediately and hastened over to the far corner table, where her daughter and husband were seated. They both rose to greet her, and Claudia permitted herself to be hugged and kissed.

Mrs. Nichols spoke in half-finished sentences, touching Claudia again and again to make sure she was real, saying how happy she was and how thin Claudia looked.

"But I'm fine, Mom. I really am." Claudia's long lashes veiled her eyes. "I'm sorry," she said, when they were seated again, "that I caused such a disturbance. I suppose I should have called you earlier, but I wasn't ready."

"We won't talk about it now," Mrs. Nichols said firmly. The next minute, however, she was saying, "It was the longest three weeks in my life. Where did you stay? Did you have enough to eat? You're sure you're all right?"

"I stayed with some kids. I had plenty to eat."

"What do you want now?" Mr. Nichols asked, motioning to a waiter. "Order anything you want."

Claudia said she was hungry and asked for a steak. Mrs. Nichols said she was too excited to eat and ordered a chef's salad, while Mr. Nichols joined Claudia in a steak. The three of them kept glancing at each other. They were like three people who had been shipboard acquaintances and were having an uneasy reunion, not able to pick up the daily threads that had bound them together during the voyage.

"I saw you on television yesterday," Claudia said.

Her mother laughed nervously. "Oh, that program. I hardly knew what I was saying, I was so upset about you. You were gone over a week when it was taped. But what an odd thing, for you to be watching TV in the morning." Her eyes were big with curiosity.

"You seemed very calm. I just happened to turn it on."

"We should call Edward," Mr. Nichols said. "He'll want to know Claudia's okay."

"My God, yes. You know we had the police, we had everyone looking for you. David, tell Edward to come home. We should have a family reunion."

Claudia's face paled. "Wait. Don't call him yet."

Mr. Nichols, halfway out of his seat, sat back down. "What's the matter? Do you feel all right?"

"Yes. . . ." Her voice was very low. "I'd better tell you. I'm not coming home. I'm staying in New York. I have a job and an apartment," she added, her face lighting up.

Both her parents stared in astonishment. "Well, I'll be damned." Mr. Nichols's face showed some admiration. "In three weeks, a job and an apartment."

"But you can't live in New York alone, if you are alone," Mrs. Nichols said. "And, besides, you have to finish high school. This is your last term."

"I don't want to finish high school now." Claudia didn't glamorize either her apartment or her job, but told them frankly that they were both less than ordinary.

Mrs. Nichols kept shaking her head while Claudia spoke. "I don't understand it. What for? How can you give up everything you have—your lovely home, your schooling—for what you say is nothing. Darling, I don't think you're telling us the whole story. Is there a boy behind this?"

"Well, I have a friend, but not what you think. He's a marvelous boy and a really great friend. He lent me money when my pocketbook was stolen." She only told them that some boys had grabbed her pocketbook and money. "And one of the reasons I called you was that I need to borrow forty dollars, just until I get paid," she added hurriedly. "I'll pay you back some each week."

Mrs. Nichols was getting edgy. "You mean, you wouldn't have called us if you didn't need the money?"

Claudia gave her mother an agonized look. "I didn't mean it that way, but it is why I needed to meet you now. You see, I had to pay the first month's rent, and my job's just starting, and also I have to lay out for the furniture."

"The whole thing's ridiculous," Mrs. Nichols said. "You're coming home with us and finishing school."

"You can't make me." Claudia's lips were trembling.

"Let's all calm down and talk this over quietly." Mr. Nichols looked from one to the other. "I suppose we could make you, if we wanted to—you're still very young, Claudia—but let's talk first and find out more about where you're living and where you intend to work."

Mr. and Mrs. Nichols did most of the talking. They pleaded earnestly, Mr. Nichols emphasizing the need for Claudia to have her high-school diploma. Later he suggested that if she wanted to stay in New York, she could live with her grandmother. With tears streaming down her cheeks, Mrs. Nichols begged Claudia to come home.

"I don't want to live with Grandma. You don't understand. I can take care of myself. You left home," Claudia said to her mother accusingly. "Why can't I?"

"That was different." Mrs. Nichols tightened her lips. "I had no opportunities."

Claudia moved restlessly in her chair. The restaurant was becoming stifling. "Excuse me, I have to go to the ladies' room." She got up, and immediately her mother followed her.

Mrs. Nichols closed the door of the small room behind them. She took off her hat and made a show of arranging her hair. "Darling, tell me about the boy you mentioned. Is he nice? What does he do?"

"He goes to NYU." Claudia ran a comb through her hair.

"I don't suppose we could meet him?"

"He's very busy. He's just a friend, Mother."

Mrs. Nichols turned away from the mirror with a frown. "Claudia, you're being very difficult. I'm not so sure you're telling us everything. I may as well be frank. Are you living with this boy?"

"No, Mother, I am not living with him. I told you I have an apartment of my own."

"The whole thing is preposterous," Mrs. Nichols said, shaking her head.

"Can we go and look at this apartment you're talking about?" Mr. Nichols asked, back at the table.

"It's nothing very much. Just a place to sleep."

"I'm not saying we're going to let you stay, but let's take a look at the apartment." Mr. Nichols asked the waiter for their check.

When the taxi drew up in front of the shabby tenement, the kids and old men and women on the street stared at the girl in the jeans, the woman in the fur coat, and the man in the fur hat who got out. Even the taxi driver's eyes widened with surprise. "Is this the place you want?"

"We'll have to walk up four flights of stairs," Claudia said.

"These halls are certainly smelly," Mrs. Nichols said, stopping to rest at the top of the second flight. "And the stairs are so steep."

"I don't mind them," Claudia said defensively.

"It certainly isn't much," Mr. Nichols commented.

"Depressing," Mrs. Nichols said.

"Sh-sh." Claudia motioned to them to be silent. The girl who was leaving the apartment had come to the door, and she was watching Claudia and her parents come up the stairs with a mocking look in her eyes.

Mrs. Nichols was at the window, looking out at the dark courtyard. "You'll never get any sun."

Claudia pointed to a geranium pot on someone's windowsill opposite. "I can look out on flowers and get some of my own if I want." In a whisper to her father, she said, "I told her I'd give her the money for the furniture today. She's leaving, and I want to move in. Can you give it to me?"

Mr. Nichols's eyes met his wife's. "I hate to be stampeded this way, but I suppose we'll have to let her try it."

"At least, let me call up a maid service and have them give the place a good cleaning. There may be bugs here."

"Mother, please!" Claudia glanced over her shoulder nervously, but the girl's back was to them, and apparently she was paying no attention. "I don't want a maid service. Please, let me do things my own way. If you'll lend me forty dollars, I'd appreciate it very much."

"What are you getting for it?" Mrs. Nichols looked around the tiny apartment.

"Most of what's here. The bed, the kitchen stuff, the chairs."

"I've got loads of pots I can give you. And a lovely set of dishes we never use. . . ."

"I don't want them. What's here is fine."

"I doubt it's worth forty dollars. That's a lot of money for this. . . ." Mrs. Nichols stopped short of saying the word *junk*. "If you weren't in such a hurry we could fix this place up together. With wallpaper and paint, new curtains, a few attractive bright pieces of furniture. . . ."

"I don't want you to fix it up. I like it the way it is. If I want to change it later I will." Claudia looked to her father. "I hate to keep asking you for the money, but if I could pay up we could leave. I'm sure we're in the way."

With a gloomy face Mr. Nichols took out his wallet. Carefully he counted out four ten-dollar bills and handed them to Claudia. Then he put five more tens in her hand. "You'd better take this. You'll need a few things."

"I don't need any more money, really I don't. I'd rather not, Dad."

"Please, I'll feel better if you have a little in reserve. Buy yourself a few good meals."

Claudia held the money irresolutely. She didn't want it, but she knew her father would be hurt and upset if she didn't take it. With a sigh she stuck the bills into her jeans pocket. "I'll buy myself a new pocketbook," she said, with forced gaiety. "Thank you."

Out on the street the good-byes were dispensed with quickly.

"What about your clothes?" Mrs. Nichols glanced with despair at Claudia's old coat and jeans. "Will you come up this weekend and pick out what you need?"

"I don't know. I'll call you." Claudia was evasive. "I'd like to get my record player sometime."

"And call your brother. Promise me, you'll call Edward."

"Yes, I'll call Edward." Claudia kissed them each good-bye and waved from the street as her parents got into a cab.

Mr. and Mrs. Nichols sat in the taxi holding hands silently. Neither one of them wanted to return to work, and they didn't speak until they got on the train for home. "I'm worried sick about her. She looks so thin and pale. And that horrid apartment. I don't think we should have let her stay."

"We didn't have much choice," Mr. Nichols said. "If we forced her to come back, she'd only go away again."

"Maybe when she comes home for the weekend, we can talk to her. . . . Persuade her to stay."

"I doubt it, but we can try. I'd like to see her finish school."

The house was emptier than ever, and the Nicholses sat through a morose, almost silent dinner. The only conversation they had was telling Anna that they had seen Claudia. Mrs. Nichols made an effort to brighten up when she spoke of her daughter. "She has a job in a little shop, and a cute apartment in the village. It's away from the street, facing a courtyard with some flowers. . . ." In her mind's eye she was turning Claudia's apartment into something she could describe to Helen Matthews.

Mr. Nichols looked at his wife in amazement. Mrs. Nichols was smiling bravely, selecting the pleasant from the unbearable, and in her own fashion reshaping the details to lighten the pain.

When I left them I felt as if I wanted to fly. Everything was set. The furniture was paid for, my first month's rent was taken care of, and I'd start the job the next day. I flew over to Steve to tell him the good news.

"Good girl," was all he said, and when he kissed me I felt that I was being born again.

I asked Steve to walk with me to Shawn and Bolten's studio, so I could collect my few things, and together we went outside. We walked hand in hand, and the whole world seemed to belong to us. The neighborhood was just as dingy as before, but it was our neighborhood. The little candy store was where I would buy my morning paper, the man in the fish market and the butcher would get to know me, the co-op would become familiar, and I'd bring home my groceries from there. I even spied a paint store where I would buy the paint for my apartment.

My apartment, my job, my boyfriend, my neighborhood. For once I knew where I was. Not all the clothes, nor furniture, nor cars, nor maids, nor anything.had ever made me feel so rich. I was the richest girl in the world, but the only thing anyone could rob me of was the fifty dollars my father had given me. I felt the money as a burden, a hangover from another life.

"Let's do something wild with my money." I showed Steve the fifty dollars. And then I remembered I owed him the money for the rent. But he said we should spend it now.

We went into a used-clothing store and bought ourselves two marvelous crazy long fur coats. Then I bought a beautiful bird and a cage, and we had enough left over for a feast for supper. When the money was spent I felt marvelous, better even than before, and together Steve and I took my things, and my new bird up to my apartment. The girl had left, and the keys were with the janitor. "I'll cook dinner for us tonight," I told Steve, and I knew it would be the best meal the two of us had ever eaten.

We had a celebration. A farewell dinner to the old, and a hailing of the new. "You are beautiful," Steve said, and he made me feel it was true.

HILA COLMAN was born and grew up in New York City, where she went to the Calhoun School. After graduation, she attended Radcliffe College. Before she started writing for herself, she wrote publicity material and ran a book club. About fourteen years ago she sold her first story to the *Saturday Evening Post*, and since then her stories and articles have appeared in many periodicals. Some have been dramatized for television. In recent years she has turned to writing books for teen-age girls. One of them, *The Girl from Puerto Rico*, was given a special citation by the Child Study Association of America.

Mrs. Colman and her husband live in Bridgewater, Connecticut. They have two sons, one of whom is married.